He had been told his contact would arrange the right time period, and make sure he could do his job with a minimum of fuss.

Everything would be timed to the second.

He could call it off, he supposed.

But this one would be the pinnacle of his career—not just in money, but in audacity.

The Crown Jewels.

Not all of them of course. But the minor ones, the ones no one had done much more than stare at under glass for hundreds of years, he could take any one of those.

If he decided to do this.

1674—July.

He thought he'd covered all the possible opportunities to steal the jewels in the 17th century.

What had he missed?

ALSO BY KRISTINE KATHRYN RUSCH

THE DIVING SERIES

Diving into the Wreck: A Diving Novel

City of Ruins: A Diving Novel

Becalmed: A Diving Universe Novella

The Application of Hope: A Diving Universe Novella

Boneyards: A Diving Novel

Skirmishes: A Diving Novel

The Runabout: A Diving Novel

The Falls: A Diving Universe Novel

Searching for the Fleet: A Diving Novel

The Spires of Denon: A Diving Universe Novella

The Renegat: A Diving Universe Novel

Escaping Amnthra: A Diving Universe Novella

The Court-Martial of the Renegat Renegades

Thieves: A Diving Novel

Squishy's Teams: A Diving Universe Novel

The Chase: A Diving Novel

Maelstrom: A Diving Universe Novella

THE RETRIEVAL ARTIST SERIES

The Disappeared

Extremes

Consequences

Buried Deep

Paloma

Recovery Man

The Recovery Man's Bargain

Duplicate Effort

The Possession of Paavo Deshin

Anniversary Day

Blowback

A Murder of Clones

Search & Recovery

The Peyti Crisis

Vigilantes

Starbase Human

Masterminds

The Impossibles

The Retrieval Artist

Writing as Kris Nelscott

THE SMOKEY DALTON SERIES

A Dangerous Road

Smoke-Filled Rooms

Thin Walls

Stone Cribs

War at Home

Days of Rage

Street Justice

AND

Protectors

_____

Writing as Kristine Grayson

The Charming Trilogy, Vol. 1

The Charming Trilogy, Vol. 2

The Fates Trilogy

The Daughters of Zeus Trilogy

THE TOWER

KRISTINE KATHRYN RUSCH

WMG
PUBLISHING

The Tower
Copyright © 2024 by Kristine Kathryn Rusch
First published in *Asimov's SF Magazine,* March, 2010.
Published by WMG Publishing
Cover and Layout copyright © 2024 by WMG Publishing
Cover art copyright © samot | Depositphotos

ISBN-13 (trade paperback): 978-1-56146-952-9
ISBN-13 (hardcover): 978-1-56146-953-6

THE TOWER

THE TOWER

THE TOWER

He had gotten a message.

Sent by old-fashioned tradecraft dating from the days of the Secret Intelligence Service, long before the advent of MI6. A simple flowerpot on a balcony in Kensington, a tiny red flag next to the ugliest flower Thomas had ever seen.

The flower didn't matter. The flag did.

It meant: *Be at the designated spot, midnight.* Be prepared.

So Thomas stood on London Bridge, his back to the traffic, his arms resting on the railing. To his left, the lights of Southwark Cathedral. To his right, the Monument designed by Sir Christopher Wren to remind everyone of the Great Fire of London in 1666.

Thomas pretended to contemplate the lights of London

reflected on the water. A bit of a wind brushed his cheeks, bringing the slightly bitter scent of the Thames.

Behind him, cars hummed as they glided by. Someone would notice him sooner or later. A man standing on London Bridge at midnight, his arms resting on the edge, looking down at the water, spoke of melancholy at the very least, a potential suicide at the very worst.

His hair ruffled as the breeze grew stronger.

Then he felt someone at his shoulder and he braced himself so that he couldn't be tossed over. His heart was pounding.

Paranoia, that's all it was. He was here to do a job, not to be killed.

Still, he stepped slightly to his left, just enough to take him out of harm's way.

"Lovely night." The voice was husky, unfamiliar—and surprisingly—female.

Thomas looked at her out of the corner of his eye. She was slight, hair cropped short, rounded cheeks reddened from the chill breeze. Maybe thirty, maybe younger.

"I've seen better." He spoke the coded response, half expecting her to go off script. After all, it was a lovely night, and strangers occasionally said such things to each other, even at midnight on London Bridge.

"I saw better on New Year's," she said. "The way the fireworks seemed to float through the Eye."

She *was* his contact then. Somehow he had always

imagined the insider was a man. Middle-aged, disgruntled. Willing to be bought off. Thomas had been watching all of them—those that he could, anyway—wondering who would meet him when the time came.

Odd that he missed a woman. Maybe that's why he had. She seemed shadowy, inconspicuous, perfect for this kind of corporate espionage.

"These days," he said, "fireworks remind me of Guy Fawkes Day when I was a boy."

"Shame they can't blow up Parliament today." She turned toward him and grinned.

He didn't grin back, but he did check, out of the corner of his eye, to see if anyone approached. Aside from the cars humming behind them, the Bridge was empty.

"So?" he asked. "You have a date certain?"

"Two, actually," she said. "The first is Wednesday at five p.m. West Wall, White Tower. The second is July, 1674."

"1674?" he asked. "I don't want that year."

"It's your only hope," she said. "They don't like doing remotes. You're lucky. The researcher is highly regarded, but female. She doesn't dare walk across the Thames. She has to be on location."

He shook his head. "I want 1650, early September 1666, or 9 May 1671. 1674 is too late."

"You've also made your impatience known," she said. "If you want to finish your job in the next year, you'll take 1674. It's the only remote planned."

"They're not doing other remotes?" He certainly wouldn't hear of them. He did work at Portals, just like this woman did, but he had never been assigned to the technical areas. The managers had actually given tests to all applicants, and he had failed the mathematical portions. But he had aced the history sections. So he'd spent the past two years in research, finding out tiny things for major historians, and growing more and more impatient.

"They're afraid of remotes. They've only done one, and it was controlled. This is the first uncontrolled remote, and some think it too dangerous."

"Uncontrolled?" he asked.

"Into a site where they don't know each and every detail. They don't even have the government's permission." She was staring at the Thames.

He did too, watching the lights ripple on the inky black water. He could get caught on this end, then, not by Portales, but by the British government. But there were no laws against time travel. Not yet.

"You have to be careful," she said as if reading his thoughts. "This is the first such major experiment. Try not to cock it up."

Cock it up. As if he were part of the corporate team. He didn't care if they never had another remote, so long as he got his treasure.

But he wasn't sure how he would go about it, even with this remote. "What happened in July of 1674?"

4

The woman didn't answer. Instead, she stared at the Thames for a moment. Then she said, "You're the fake historian. You figure it out. And, by the way, your portal is Neyla Kendrick. Good luck."

His portal. A pun. He hated puns, and was about to tell her when he realized she was walking away from him. The breeze carried her vanilla perfume long after her footsteps faded.

He had been told his contact would arrange the right time period, and make sure he could do his job with a minimum of fuss. Everything would be timed to the second.

He needed it timed. He needed it just so.

He could call it off, he supposed. His client would hire someone else, someone with less caution, someone with a few more balls.

Not that he lacked balls. He'd carried out some of the greatest thefts in living memory.

But this one would be the pinnacle of his career—not just in money, but in audacity.

The Crown Jewels.

Not all of them of course. The most famous ones as well as the ones still in use had to remain. But the minor ones, the ones he'd researched, the ones no one had done much more than stare at under glass for hundreds of years, he could take any one of those, and would.

If he decided to do this.

5

1674—July.

He thought he'd covered all the possible opportunities to steal the jewels in the 17th century.

What had he missed?

———

T he thick linen tape actually put pressure on her chest. Neyla Kendrick had trouble drawing a breath.

"That's too tight," she said to McTavish, who was trying to dress her.

The Closet was cold. Rows of clothing, all on racks, all from different time periods, ran off into the distance.

She felt like she was in one of the old warehouses that used to line this part of Southwark after the Second World War. She had to remind herself that beyond the double doors was a modern well-lit hallway.

McTavish tugged at the tape one more time.

"That *hurts*," she said.

He let go and the tape unraveled. She took a deep breath for the first time since he had wrapped the stuff around her. She looked down. Red welts covered the fleshy part of her upper breasts.

"Just get the reduction," McTavish said. "You can have them inflated when you get back."

As if her breasts were balloons. She glared at him.

McTavish had been a dresser, a costumer, and finally a designer for the London Stage. Portals, Inc. had hired him away with an obscene salary, mostly for his knowledge of historical fashion. Not just because he knew how to make someone look like they were from, say, the Middle Ages, but because he could actually pinpoint a year. He could find or make materials that fit so accurately, no native of the time period would think anything was wrong.

McTavish wasn't that careful with his own clothing. He wore the standard long frock coat—this season's current design for the fashionable man—but his was velvet, and too hot. He always smelled faintly of sweat.

"I'm not going to get my breasts reduced," Neyla said. "I'm leaving Wednesday morning."

"It's cosmetic," he said. "It'll be done in less than an hour. You'll have no pain at all. And when you get back—"

"They have to put some substance inside my breasts. It won't be me any more. I like having the original equipment."

He raised his eyebrows at her. "You also want to do your research, right? With those honkers, no one's going to mistake you for a boy, not unless I wrap all of your torso."

"I won't be bathing," she said, still shuddering at the very idea. She was going back to the land of unwashed flesh, fleas, and bedbugs. That was what she feared the most. The bugs, the dirt, the way she would have to live it all.

"It'll be July," McTavish said. "Hottest month of the year in any century. You'll already be wearing more clothing than you're accustomed to. The last thing I want is for you to get heatstroke. Another reason not to bind these puppies. Get them reduced."

"No," she said. "You're going to flatten them and you're going to make it look natural."

Then she grabbed her pink cotton shirt and pulled it on, leaving her bra on the nearby rack as if she had forgotten it. She wasn't going to wear anything over "those puppies." She was going back to work.

"It's not going to look natural," he said.

"Neither are my teeth," she said, "but I'm not having those pulled for verisimilitude either."

Then she stalked out of the Closet.

She was getting angry at McTavish and that wasn't right. He was just a perfectionist, trying to make her the best 17th century male she could possibly be. He was trying to protect her.

She appreciated the attempt at protection. But she wasn't going to give up her breasts. She had given up enough for her work. Just moving to London was enough of a sacrifice.

She was a San Francisco girl, born and raised. She loved the cool air, the fog, the modern buildings and the lack of history. She had gotten all of her degrees at UC-Berkeley, as well as two post-docs, one assistant professorship, followed by a full professorship with summers off and tons of university support to go all over the world to investigate old bones.

She had been about to accept a tenured position when Portals, Inc. contacted her, asking her to submit a proposal for their top-secret project.

Time travel. Controlled, examined. Portals wanted to investigate all kinds of historical avenues before taking its product public. It was a giant form of beta testing. If something went wrong for the historians investigating old myths, virologists investigating ancient diseases, and biologists trying to get DNA from long-vanished species, then Portals would do more testing on its travel system.

Neyla's proposal was simple: It was a redraft of her undergraduate honors thesis, which she had written in conjunction with the History, English, and Anthropology departments. Her thesis was an analysis of the importance of the Princes in the Tower, as told by their bones. Not that she had seen their bones, of course. No one alive had. The bones had been examined only once, in 1933. What then passed for modern science concluded that the bones belonged to two young boys who were the right age to be the princes, and therefore probably were.

That conclusion was enough for the British government. Since then, they hadn't allowed anyone to examine the bones.

She hadn't expected Portals to care about the ancient

mystery of the Princes in the Tower, but apparently they had received so many requests from historians and amateur crime buffs, all of whom wanted to solve the mystery themselves (and wanted to spend a year in 1483 and 1484 doing so), that the Portals CEO, Damien Wilder, figured this could be the signature project.

He had been looking for someone who knew how to solve the mystery of the Princes' deaths in a short visit to the past. Neyla's proposal was the shortest—a return to July of 1674, when the skeletons were discovered on the south side of the White Tower. Unfortunately, no one had a date certain, so anyone hoping to find the bodies might have to spend the entire month in 1674—which was a prospect she was now facing.

She stepped inside her office, her heart pounding. She was still angry over McTavish's comment. Not because he had any power to make her go through even minor physical changes for this project, but because he had tapped into her fears about this trip.

So many risks. She had to somehow pose as one of the workers or someone who belonged at the Tower during July of 1674. She and her team would be traveling with only the minimum of supplies, a second set of clothing, and the miniaturized scientific equipment.

She slipped behind her desk. Beyond the large glass windows, London sprawled. The skyscape looked nothing like the skyscape in 1674. Then the Tower housed some of the largest buildings in the city. Now century-old buildings dwarfed it. Even the creaky London Eye made the Tower look like a hunk of the past stuck in the middle of the present.

She pulled out the box holding the equipment she would take with her. The box was long and thin as if it contained a necklace from Tiffany's. Inside were small items designed to look like things from 1674, a quill pen, a pin, a ring. They all housed something important from her computer (complete with camera and voice recorder) to the many backups she needed.

Everything was solar powered, which helped. Her traveling companions would have redundant equipment, so if someone lost theirs, they wouldn't lose the information.

The entire trip could be summed up in this small box. If she didn't get the right information at the right time in the right way, the trip and all its dangers would be for nothing.

She couldn't quite get over her own audacity.

To travel into one of the world's most heavily guarded places, to a place still more famous for its prisoners and executions than for its grandeur and its coronations, took a degree of chutzpah she would never have guessed that she had.

Finally she stood and walked to the window. The Thames glittered in the sunlight. Cars flowed over the bridges and through the city, like blood through veins. She was too high to see people walking. From this vantage, though, she could see the entire Tower complex from Traitor's Gate up front to the Jewel House toward the back and the White Tower in the very middle.

Dark and old, foreboding and entrancing, the Tower at this moment was filled with tourists and schoolchildren, people who had paid to "experience" the past.

In two days, she would join them, pretending to be that peculiar kind of tourist who dressed up in period dress to enjoy an historical monument.

In two days, she would stand by the White Tower, and become someone else.

————

Neyla Kendrick was exactly the kind of person Thomas didn't want to travel with. One of those esoteric scientific types with a narrow specialty who might have to spend an entire month in the past for one moment alone with a pile of bones.

Thomas wanted to get in and get out, quick and dirty. He'd been willing to spend a few days in September of 1666, the Great Fire, just to get the right opportunity. But even his vaguer instructions for the Cromwellian era took into account the fact that the Jewels weren't very important in the Interregnum. Most got sold or lost or stolen.

Thomas had just planned to do a bit of the stealing, in a very short period of time.

Now he had to spend a month with a woman interested in the bones of children. He wasn't even sure what the fuss was about. The Princes had died hundreds of years ago, at a time when England routinely killed its monarchs. It wasn't even accurate to call the boys princes. Technically, one—Edward—was the King of England.

The son of Edward IV, Edward V's only crime was being underage and sickly. His brother Richard was the spare to the heir.

They had come to the Tower voluntarily, to prepare for Edward's reign. His uncle Richard was supposed to be the kid's Protector, the person who managed the Kingdom until the boy came of age. But something happened—historical crap no one really cared about any more—and Richard (the uncle not the spare) decided to take the Kingship for himself.

The boys lived for a while after Richard took the throne. And eventually they died—either from sickness or murder most foul. Richard became the infamous Richard the Third, known more for murdering his nephews than for his deeds as King.

Had the boys been allowed to rule, the entire history of the English monarchy might have changed.

But they hadn't been allowed to rule, and there were more than enough murders after them. Henry VIII murdered wives, for heaven's sake. His eldest daughter became known as Bloody Mary for her actions as Queen of

England and his youngest daughter, Elizabeth, had been no shrinking violet.

Every English monarch of the period killed "pretenders" to the throne, some of whom had more claim to that throne than the person sitting in it.

And each death, if prevented, could have changed the course of English history.

So...two little boys? Really, who cared?

The biggest problem Thomas had wasn't with Neyla Kendrick or with the long-lost Princes. It was with his own knowledge base. He was going to replace one of Kendrick's assistants.

Thomas knew everything there was to know about the Tower during the Great Fire. He also knew everything he could possibly learn about Thomas Blood, whose attempt to steal the Crown Jewels on 9 May 1671 was one of the more famous thefts in English history.

Thomas even knew which Jewels were lost forever in the Interregnum.

He just didn't know what had joined the collection by 1674, what would be missed, and what wouldn't.

With only less than two days to find out, he didn't have time to study. This job was becoming a great deal of aggravation.

But, he had to remind himself, no amount of aggravation would make him quit.

There was no better target than this one, no better test of his skills.

To commit the crime of a lifetime took an amazing thief.

To commit the crime of several lifetimes took one of the best thieves ever.

He wanted that title for his own.

———

"He's *what?*" Neyla asked. "He's *sick?* That's not possible. Men like Peter Wilson don't get sick."

The flunky half bowed as Neyla spoke. He was scrawny, with bad teeth, and thinning hair. And he was *young*, twenty-two if he was a day. She had never seen him before, but then she hadn't seen half the people who worked for Portals before. Because he was afraid to give her bad news himself, the head of Travel had sent this poor soul to her. Apparently, the head of Travel had figured out she'd be pissed off.

"Beg pardon, ma'am," the flunky said timidly, "but Dr. Wilson's got pneumonia. He nearly died. One of his lungs collapsed. They've reinflated it and given him some kind of treatment, but he won't be well by tomorrow at five—at least not well enough to trust him alone without medical help in such a primitive time. Ma'am."

15

"You'd think in this day and age," she said, "no one would ever get that sick."

"Beg pardon, Ma'am," the flunky said, "but people still do get ill on occasion."

"But pneumonia? None of us should've gotten that. It's one of those things that can be prevented." She ran a hand through her hair. "This makes no sense. Pete Wilson is our biologist, our food specialist. He's the one who is supposed to prevent *us* from getting sick. He can't get sick himself, not before we go."

The flunky wisely remained silent.

"I suppose we have to call this off now." She stood, turned her back on the flunky, and went to the window. The Tower looked foreboding in the sunlight.

She half expected to feel relief, but she felt none. She wanted to go, and she wanted to go tomorrow.

"I've been told, Ma'am, that no one wants to cancel. They've assigned you someone else."

She frowned. "They've assigned...?"

She had handpicked Pete, just like she had picked the rest of her team. But her contract did give Portals the right to assign people to her team. She had argued about that, and she had lost. Portals wanted the right to send troubleshooters and others on trips to take care of potential problems.

"His name is Thomas Ayliffe," the flunky said, "and—"

"Bullshit." She turned. "They're not sending someone

named Thomas Ayliffe to the Tower of London in 1674. They can't be serious."

The flunky's cheeks had turned red. "I'm not in charge —I mean, what's wrong with Thomas Ayliffe?"

"You're clearly not up on your 17th century London history," she snapped. "Who assigned this idiot to my team?"

"Mr. Wycroft, at least he's the one who told me—"

She didn't need any more. She pushed past the flunky and stormed to Wycroft's lair.

Wycroft had half of the entire twentieth floor. He had assistants everywhere. He was nominally Neyla's boss, although she really answered to Darien Wilder.

Wycroft's receptionist was an old battle-ax who had been hired away from one of Britain's stuffiest banks. She had been hired for her prim and proper attitude, and her withering looks.

But Neyla could out-wither anyone. She took one look at the battle-ax, and the woman leaned back, ceding the field. Neyla hurried past her, only to be joined by Wycroft's chief assistant, Flynn Martin.

He was short and stocky with a friendly face and dark hair just starting to go gray. People mistook him for an easy-going person, but Neyla knew better. Flynn Martin was the steel inside Wycroft's velvet glove.

"I know you're upset," Flynn said. "But, Neyla, we need this trip to go off tomorrow—"

"I'm not taking any old person along with me because you have a schedule." Neyla kept moving, past desks and fake plants and tasteful copies of sculptures from London's most famous monuments.

"We need to test the remote devices," Flynn said. "We've put a lot of planning into this—"

"So have I," Neyla said, "and I'm not going to let some idiot get in my way and blow my cover on the very first afternoon."

"Neyla, let's talk like adults—"

"Yes, let's," she said. "And since my problem is with Harrison Wycroft, I'll speak to him, not to you."

She slammed both hands against the double doors leading into Wycroft's office. The doors banged open.

Wycroft sat behind his desk, with his back to the floor-to-ceiling windows. The cityscape extended beyond him, almost as if it were a decoration in his office, the London Eye turning lazily to his right.

"Neyla," Wycroft said without saying hello, "he's the only person we have available with at least a passing knowledge of the 17th Century."

Wycroft was an obese man whose size seemed appropriate, partly because he favored three-piece black bespoke suits, bowler hats, and the ubiquitous black umbrella.

"So postpone the trip until Pete is well," Neyla said.

Wycroft sighed and waved a hand at Flynn. Flynn pulled the doors closed as he stepped back outside.

"Pete, it seems, isn't as cautious as we thought. He was dealing with bacteria from another trip, this one to the 15th century, and comparing various disease vectors, somehow infecting himself with a particularly virulent strain of Pneumocystis carinii. The problem is that he's ill and in isolation, and we're not going to get him back for weeks, maybe months. Even then he might not be cleared to travel."

She crossed her arms. "How long has he been ill?"

"He's had a cough for a week. It got worse over the weekend."

"And no one thought to warn me?"

"We hoped it wouldn't be serious."

She shook her head. She understood why Pete wasn't going. She even understood the need for haste with this trip. Portals had its various patents to protect, experiments to foster, research and development to promote. She was only one small cog in a very big wheel.

What she didn't understand was how no one seemed to understand that a man named Thomas Ayliffe would be a problem.

"This Thomas Ayliffe is pulling your chain," she said.

"What's wrong with Ayliffe?" Wycroft asked. "Have you had difficulty with him before?"

"What's wrong with him?" she snapped, stepping toward Wycroft. "What's *wrong* with him? You say he's an expert on 17th century London."

"The closest that we have on such short notice, yes," Wycroft said.

"If he's an expert," she said, "he's giving you a message. Have you done an identity check on this man?"

Wycroft slid out a drawer. He pressed something—probably one of his private networked computer links—and examined the answer.

"Yes, of course. He went through the same rather difficult vetting system that you did."

"His name is legitimate?" she asked.

"Yes." The answer came from behind her.

Neyla turned. A man stood there. He was tall, broad-shouldered, and as well dressed as Wycroft, only in a suit that wasn't half as conservative. The man had black hair, blue eyes, and ruggedly handsome features.

"I don't believe we've been introduced." His British accent was so posh that he sounded like he belonged at Buckingham Palace. "I'm Thomas Ayliffe."

"And I'm Nellie Bly," she said.

He stared at her with that same withering look that the battle-ax outside had perfected. "You can check my birth records."

"We have," Wycroft said. "Neyla, what's your objection to the man's name?"

"Apparently Ms. Kendrick believes I'm going to use the name when we go to 1674. And that would be unwise." Ayliffe walked into the room, stopping beside her. He smelled of soap, as if he had just stepped out of the shower.

She looked at him sideways. He was significantly taller than she was, which was also a problem. Brits in the 17th century, especially working class Brits, were notably short due to poor nutrition and unhealthy environmental conditions.

"You see," Ayliffe said, "Thomas Ayliffe was one of the many names used by the infamous Thomas Blood."

"Why is that a familiar name?" Wycroft asked.

"For god's sake," Neyla said. "Thomas Blood is the most famous person ever to steal the Crown Jewels."

Wycroft stared at her.

"In 1671. He failed, but spectacularly," she said. "He became a folk hero, depending on your political persuasion at the time. Remember, Cromwell was only a few years before, and not everyone believed in the restoration of the monarchy."

Wycroft raised his eyebrows.

"I can't help my family name," Ayliffe said, "but I promise not to use it when we travel. It's not like you need a passport anyway. No one checks your identification."

Neyla glared at him. He didn't even look at her. He directed all of his comments to Wycroft, which she also found irritating.

But she could do the same thing. "He's too tall," she said.

"Both Henry Tudors were over six feet," Ayliffe said.

"Henry the Seventh and his son, Henry the Eighth, were both royalty raised in the best of conditions. Besides, by 1674, they were long dead. No one would remember that they were tall. They would simply remember that Henry VIII was supremely fat."

She bit her lip, wishing she hadn't said that in front of Wycroft. She made herself continue, partly to cover her gaffe. She now turned toward Ayliffe.

"Even if they did remember how tall the Henries were," she said, "you're going to be posing as some ditch digger who probably never had real meat or fresh vegetables in his entire life. You'll stand out."

"And you won't?" He finally turned to her, then he let his gaze run up and down her entire figure.

To her own disgust, she blushed. She wasn't going to defend her appearance.

"According to his file," Wycroft said, "Mr. Ayliffe here used to participate in the Society for Creative Anachronism, so he's not averse to costuming. He works in our history department, specializing in the Elizabethan era, which isn't that much different from the era you'll be traveling in—"

"It's different enough," Neyla snapped.

"But the clothing and customs are close," Wycroft said.

"Close isn't good enough," she said. "We've been working on this for two years. We have a team."

"Pete's not going no matter how you argue it," Wycroft said. "And waiting won't help. We're just going to have to muddle through."

"Let's muddle through without the tall guy," she said. "The rest of us are ready. I don't know what he'll add."

"I do know something about food," Ayliffe said. "I spent a few years at Stratford before I realized that acting wasn't for me, so 17th century English isn't that foreign to me. I will probably be able to understand the natives better than you will."

He had a point, although she wasn't going to concede it. Everyone who studied with the Royal Shakespeare Company spent quite a bit of time learning how to speak Elizabethan English, which was still what they were speaking in the 1670s. Her American accent was going to be a handicap. She had planned to speak to the locals as little as possible.

"You will need a translator, right?" Ayliffe asked. "And I didn't see one on your list. I think that might be a lot more valuable than a biologist."

"Pete isn't just a biologist," she said. "He was in charge of food safety."

"If you want safe food, stay here," Ayliffe said. "Back there, you're going to eat things that horrify you because you have no other choice. You'll just have to trust that all those medical precautions they took here at Portals will protect you."

"Nothing will protect against food poisoning," she said.

"Expect a mild case or two," he said. "I've had it. It's not pleasant, but you'll survive."

"In the modern era," she said. "Four hundred years ago, it could kill you."

"But we'll have the remotes," he said. "We'll be able to come back if someone gets deathly ill. Right?"

He directed that last question to Wycroft.

Wycroft's mouth pursed. His eyes shifted to Neyla, then back to Ayliffe. Wycroft looked very uncomfortable.

So no one had briefed Ayliffe on all of the details. Just some of them.

Ayliffe looked from Wycroft to Neyla. "What don't I know?"

"We can return any time in the first three days," she said. "Then we have another window thirty days later. That's it."

"What do you mean, that's it?"

She shrugged. "If we miss the windows, there's a very good chance we'll get stuck back there."

She tried to sound calm about it, but she wasn't calm. She was going to monitor those windows like nothing else, and she was going to return in one of them, no matter what.

"Why?" Ayliffe asked. "You can come back any time. Time travel is time travel is time travel. It doesn't correlate. Even if you leave the past on 30 July 1674, you'll be able to arrive back here one second after you left. What's the problem?"

"It's a design flaw in the remotes," Wycroft said. "Something we haven't been able to solve yet."

"Whatever the remotes do," Neyla said, being as vague as she could be since she never really bothered to understand the science, "they work on the initial energy burst for the first three days. Then the system will go dark for a while, recharging, for lack of a better phrase. Our first opportunity to return will be in thirty days."

"Our first," Ayliffe said. "So you won't get stuck."

"We don't know that," she said. "What we do know is that only people who have used the three-day and thirty-day windows have returned. No one else has. I would assume they've tried every thirty days after that. I don't know for certain."

He frowned, then looked at Wycroft. "How do you know this? I thought this is the first major remote trip."

"You think we didn't test the remotes?" Wycroft asked. "We've been testing them for a decade."

"And you're willing to go with this design flaw?" Ayliffe sounded shocked. That pleased Neyla. Maybe he'd back out.

"It's no more dangerous than sending someone back to the 17th century," Wycroft said in that tone he used when he was spouting corporate cover-your-assisms. Neyla had heard these arguments before. In fact, she had made some of them.

"So those people who got lost," Ayliffe said, "you haven't sent teams after them?"

"Where would we look?" Wycroft asked. "And what if the problem isn't the remotes? What if they got arrested or something else happened?"

"You don't leave people behind," Ayliffe said.

"They knew the risks," Wycroft said. "So do we. There's a chance that they wanted to stay, you know. Maybe they found true love."

He couldn't hide the sarcasm from his voice. Since Portals went public, the number of movies and novels about people finding love back in time had quadrupled.

"Most likely they died," Neyla said.

Ayliffe looked at her, obviously alarmed.

Neyla added, "If you come with us—and I think you shouldn't—you're not going to go on some sanctioned SCA field trip or some little practice holiday for Elizabethan scholars. You'll be entering a dark, dirty world more dangerous than any third world country. The longer we stay, the less chance we have of surviving."

"So let's get in and out fast," Ayliffe said.

"We can't," she said. "I don't know what day in July they discovered the bodies of the Princes. Even if I did know, I'm not sure how fast I'll be able to gain access to them."

"This is," Wycroft said, "our first experiment in a deliberately long trip. We've had accidentally long trips in the past, but not something like this."

Ayliffe visibly swallowed. He looked nervous for the first time since she had met him.

"And," Neyla said, mostly to make him more nervous, "most of those accidentally long trips happened in the time travel booth here in Portals itself. Remotes aren't the only problem with time travel."

Ayliffe studied her. Then he squared his shoulders, and looked at Wycroft.

"I suppose I have to sign waivers," Ayliffe said.

Wycroft looked relieved. For some reason, he seemed to want Ayliffe on this trip. "You'll also have to go to medical and make certain you're both healthy enough for the trip and you have the right protections."

Ayliffe nodded, then he tipped an imaginary hat to Neyla. "Nice meeting you," he said. "Looks like we'll be spending some time together."

"Not if I can help it," she said.

———

Thomas left. He hadn't expected this much resistance. He had spent two years building his cover at Portals, making certain his identity was rock-solid and unimpeachable, and his work record perfect.

He hadn't known his allies in the company would deliberately make one of the original team ill, but it made sense. He also hadn't expected anyone to know what his name meant. But then, he had initially planned on traveling back in time alone. He had been opening the door to Wycroft's office when Neyla Kendrick had said *If he's an expert, he's giving you a message*, and he damn near turned around and left.

He'd always used names like Thomas Ayliffe on jobs. A bit of an inside joke, which meant nothing to anyone but him.

But she had seen through it—and accurately. He had sent a small message, one that he hadn't expected to be received until after he left, if he had accomplished his task.

She made him nervous.

She was also too pretty to masquerade as a boy. Too pretty and too buxom. He had no idea how the costumers were going to hide those curves, but they had quite a job ahead of them.

Which reminded him. He needed clothes for the journey.

He had a lot to do before five o'clock tomorrow. He hoped he could finish everything in time.

At four o'clock on Wednesday, the team assembled in Neyla's office, dressed in appropriate clothing, all in varying shades of brown. Some of the brown had nothing to do with dye. McTavish had dragged white shirts through mud and dirt and let them dry, then tried to wash them by hand with lye soap. The shirts weren't so much brown as a kind of crap-colored dark tan.

Neyla's breasts had finally been tamed, and the wrapping didn't even hurt. McTavish, working with some of the scientists, found a nice mixture of spandex and nanotechnology to squish her breasts. Then McTavish wound some regular cloth around her belly, so that she looked like a man who had a barrel chest, rather than a pretty boy with man-boobs.

When she looked at herself in the mirror, with her short hair, barrel chest, and spindly legs, she seemed like something out of Hogarth—one of the wide-eyed commoners crowding around the subject of the drawing on crammed streets of London.

The rest of her team looked authentic too—at least to her. Jeff Renolet, who didn't need wrapping to create his own barrel chest, stood beside her. He was in his forties, balding, with a ruddy face. He normally wore crowns on his front teeth, but Portals' dentist had removed them for this trip. Jeff looked like an old fat man who had been repeatedly punched in the mouth.

29

Next to Jeff, Benedict Ivance scratched underneath one arm. He had chosen loose-weave linen, which held dirt in every single wrinkle. Modern linen had been treated so that it was soft, but linen without treatment was rough. If he was scratching already, he would be raw by the time this trip was over.

Compared to the others, Dan Sheldon looked like a half-grown boy. He was whip-thin thanks to his daily six-mile runs and his love of urban free climbing. His eyes were clear, his blond hair cut in a bowl-shape. He had the kind of innocent face that often showed up in religious paintings of the era. Instead of his filthy clothes, he should have been wearing priest's robes.

Thomas Ayliffe towered over all of them. His clothing was a bit upscale for a member of the working class, but McTavish had taken care of that by ripping it, mending it, and then ripping it again. Ayliffe looked like an elegant man who had come upon hard times.

Besides, Neyla was beginning to think the man would look good in anything.

She hated that she found him attractive. He was annoying and in the way, and he was noticeable. He was going to scotch this mission just by being part of it. She knew it, and she resented it.

She had done everything she could to get rid of him. She had spent fifteen minutes after Ayliffe left Wycroft's office, trying to convince him to take Ayliffe off the team.

When that didn't work, she had gone all the way to Damien Wilder's office, only to be told that Wilder was in Japan, making some kind of presentation.

She was stuck with elegant, good-looking Ayliffe and with his ripped upscale clothes.

Her party's cover story was simple. They had joined up on a trip to London to find work. They'd been in the city only a few months and had found just enough to keep them alive.

Theoretically, the story explained their extra clothing, their bundles of supplies and the fact that none of them looked like the other. Friends and colleagues, not relatives.

They'd had the story drummed into them, practicing it and everything else at odd moments. Neyla, the only one without a British accent, had vowed not to speak much, at least around natives. But the others had to be careful as well. Jeff had studied 17th century speech and Ayliffe knew Elizabethan English, but neither of them had heard it spoken correctly.

They double-checked their equipment one last time. Everyone had their own remote, as well as their own tiny computers. Some had specialized equipment. Ayliffe got custody of Pete's food safety devices, with a short instruction on how to use them. Because Pete wasn't coming along, Neyla insisted on double the amount of water purification tablets even if that meant a little extra bulk in their kits.

When they were done, she looked at the entire group. "Last chance to back out," she said.

They stared at her. Jeff's right eye had developed a nervous tick. Benedict bit his lower lip, as if he were trying not to say anything, and Dan took a deep breath, clearly trying to calm himself.

Only Ayliffe looked like a man about to go on an adventure. His eyes were bright, his cheeks slightly flushed.

"All right, then," she said. "Off we go."

They took a cab to the western entrance, and piled out like the excited tourists they were pretending to be. Neyla gazed up at the massive stone entrance, as impressive now as it had been the first time she had come here. Her stomach did a slight flip, and her breath caught.

Now it all felt real to her.

She followed her little troop through the arches, past the buskers and the tradesmen offering everything from a printout of that day's news to Tower trinkets supposedly for less than they were being sold for inside.

Almost no one walked in with her group. What tourists they saw were leaving. The Tower closed to visitors at six, and most people had spent all day here.

The modern gift shop looked garish in front of the

Middle Tower. Neyla walked past it to the matching ticket booths. They seemed as out of place as the gift shop, but at least they didn't block the old entrance to one of the towers.

She hurried up to the window, the other members of her team following her.

"Five tickets," she said, broadening her American accent and filling her voice with excitement.

The ticket taker, an elderly woman with a kind face, leaned toward the plastic separating her from Neyla. "Ah, luv, I've got to charge you full price, and you'll only get an hour in there. Come back tomorrow noon latest, and you'll be able to enjoy the whole place."

"I'm flying home tomorrow," Neyla lied, sounding as disappointed as she could.

The ticket taker sighed, as if this were her problem, not Neyla's. "Then you're better off, luv, walking the outside for free, taking pictures and looking at the ravens. It's a lot of money for just an hour, and I don't feel right selling you a ticket."

Just sell me a damn ticket, Neyla wanted to snap. *I'm sure your bosses would appreciate the revenue.*

But she smiled instead. "You're so kind. But my friends here want to see the Crown Jewels, and I want to see where Anne Boleyn got her head cut off."

The ticket taker winced at Neyla's crudeness, but it

33

worked. Playing the demanding American got her exactly what she wanted.

She bought five tickets, then led her little group back to the Middle Tower. The Middle Tower had been an entrance into the entire complex since the beginning of the 14th century. It had to have been impressive then, so tall and formidable and new.

Neyla knew the history of each and every building. She knew who built it and why, its various uses, and when it was remodeled, moved, or, in a few cases, destroyed. She carried multiple maps of the entire complex in her head, just in case the remotes worked improperly. The last thing she wanted was to overshoot their historical timeslot and end up inside the wall of a building that had later been torn down—or a moat that had been filled in.

Her group had quite a trek from the Middle Tower down Lanthorn Lane to the Bloody Tower, which would take them to the Inner Ward. Tourists had gone on a prescribed walk ever since the Tower was opened to the public, centuries ago.

She knew there were other ways inside the Tower's defenses, she just wasn't allowed to take those ways as a member of the public.

As her team walked, they gawked at their surroundings like proper tourists. The real tourists gawked at them, dressed in their period costume. They received several stares and more than a few people pointed at them.

Neyla tried to ignore them all. She kept her eye on the Bloody Tower, as she had since the first time she had come here. It got its name from the Princes. The Bloody Tower was the last place they'd been seen alive, looking out the windows in 1483. Over time, no one saw them any more, and Tudor historians claimed Richard III had murdered them there.

Of course, no one knew exactly what happened to the Princes, if indeed they were murdered there or anywhere else. Even if they had died there and the 1933 examination of the bodies was correct, then someone had taken the corpses and carried them across the grounds to the Innermost Ward, where they were buried in the foundation of a spiral staircase.

The bodies had been found in 1674, when workers getting rid of a forebuilding attached to the White Tower dug into the foundation of that staircase. The workers hadn't been surprised.

It wasn't unusual for bodies to be buried all over the Tower's grounds. After all, the place had served as a prison from its very beginnings over 1,000 years ago. Many times, unidentified skeletons were discovered throughout the complex; more than once, dozens of bodies were discovered at the same time.

Generally no one cared who the skeletons belonged to. The Princes were one of the few exceptions.

The team reached the Bloody Tower, but didn't stop.

Neyla didn't look at the windows like she usually did and wonder which ones had provided Edward V's last view of the world.

Now the team had entered the Inner Ward, where the Tower's most famous history occurred. Here, on these grounds, Henry VIII had conducted the beheadings of his rivals and wives. Here Elizabeth the First, when she was imprisoned in the Bell Tower by her sister Mary, walked every day with an escort, probably trying not to look at the spot where her mother had died.

"We're nuts," Jeff whispered.

"You want to back out?" she asked him, feeling a surge of disappointment.

He shook his head slowly, as if he were warring with himself. "Just didn't expect it to feel so real, you know?"

She did know. They stopped on the west side of the White Tower, the oldest building in the entire complex. William the Conqueror had built it in 1097 out of gleaming white Caen stone. It had stood alone on the banks of the Thames, a large Norman keep, the tallest building in all of England, twenty-seven meters high.

Neyla looked up all those meters. The Caen stone had held up well. It no longer gleamed, but it still looked white, partly because of the cleanings that it routinely suffered now that preservationists had decided that the filth in the air would eventually cause the stone to decay.

One of the Yeoman Warders, in his regulation Elizabethan black and red garb (tourists called the Warders Beefeaters, which made her think of gin), approached their group. He turned to Ayliffe, as if Ayliffe were their leader.

"You only have about a half hour, lad, if you're going to see anything important. We shut down promptly at six."

"Thanks," Ayliffe said. "We're nearly done."

The Warder nodded, then wandered away, probably to give his warning to the other remaining tourists.

"We'd better act fast," Dan said.

"We're going to take our time," Neyla said. Going too fast might cause mistakes. The first—and most important —thing they had to do was find the right spot on the ground outside the White Tower.

The grass had been cordoned off—too many feet would cause the stuff to stop growing—but the grass not too far from the northwest corner of the White Tower was exactly where they wanted to stand. They couldn't get anywhere near that demolished forebuilding, since no one knew exactly how big it had been.

Benedict watched the Warders. He would give the team the all clear when they could run for the grass. The rest of the team pulled out their remotes.

The remotes were thin disks that looked like badly crafted circles that hung from a chain. Only right now, no one in the group wore theirs. They were instead squeezing the disk's sides to turn it on.

The technical team already programmed the date and

time in. No one on Neyla's team knew how to program these things, even though she begged for the chance to learn back when this trip got scheduled.

She wanted to control when she returned. But she was told that the remotes were so delicate that one mistake could send her into a different time period, and strand her there forever.

She wasn't sure she believed it. Portals was a corporation after all, and divisions in corporations did their very best to hoard knowledge so that they could hoard power. But she hadn't won this argument either.

When she finished turning her device on, she took Benedict's and started it. Then she and the team waited while he watched.

Finally, he nodded. The group hurried to their spot on the grass, and when Neyla gave the signal, pressed the center of the disks, activating the travel mechanism.

She clutched her disk so hard, she was afraid she was going to break it. At first, nothing happened. She glanced over at the Bloody Tower, saw a Warder running toward them, and then he simply faded away.

Everything went completely black. A wind buffeted her, changing direction constantly. Thunder clapped—or maybe she was hearing sonic booms—and the air grew hotter, then colder, then hotter again.

For a moment, she felt like she was falling, and then she realized she really was falling. She landed in a heap on the hard ground, the wind gone, the air warm and fetid.

She blinked hard, realized the darkness wasn't quite absolute. A moon shone above her and the stars surrounded it.

She'd never been able to see the stars in London before.

"Anyone else here?" she asked quietly.

She sat up, stretched her limbs, and realized that while she didn't have any broken bones, she would be badly bruised.

Her heart was pounding.

"I'm here," Dan said, his voice as soft as hers. "Hit my head pretty hard."

Her eyes were adjusting. She could see the outlines of the White Tower now, and thought she might see a dim light through one of the windows. A dim, flickering light. A lantern, perhaps, or a candle.

"You all right?" she asked.

"I think so," he said.

She moved toward his voice. She craved real light—a flashlight, a small phone/computer display, something. She hadn't planned on the darkness.

It felt like a live thing. A close, smelly live thing. Her eyes burned. The air was filled with smoke.

She hadn't expected that either.

"Anyone else here?" she asked as she groped for Dan. Finally her hand found wool.

"Ouch," he said and pulled away. "I banged myself something awful."

"Me, too," she said.

"God. They said we'd fall. They didn't say it would be so far." That voice belonged to Benedict. "You'd think they could calculate how much dirt and fill and stuff accumulated over the centuries."

Neyla sighed in relief at hearing his voice.

"Are you all right?" she asked Benedict.

"Banged up, just like Dan, but nothing serious."

"They said we'd fall only a few decimeters. Did that seem like a few decimeters to anyone? Seemed like at least a meter to me," Dan said.

Neyla had no idea. The fall was expected but hard. She was beginning to worry that Jeff and Ayliffe were too badly injured to speak.

"Experts don't know everything." That was Jeff. He half mumbled it. "I don't think they considered the tiny details. After all, they weren't the ones traveling in time."

Neyla was relieved to hear his voice. "Any broken bones, Jeff?"

"Twisted my ankle, but I can put weight on it. I'll be all right."

All the voices were close to her. She let out a sigh. "What about you, Thomas? You okay?"

Silence. She heard her own breath, a little ragged as it

went in and out. Beside her, fabric rustled. Then someone's joint made a cracking noise.

"Thomas?" Why would Ayliffe pretend to be hurt? Why wouldn't he answer? "Feel around for him, guys. Maybe he got knocked unconscious."

She kept her voice down as she spoke. She didn't know if guards patrolled the grounds.

Clearly, her team had arrived at night. Which was good on one level—she would be able to see how far the work progressed, maybe even find the bodies herself—and bad on another. She would have to figure out what to do with her team before dawn, whether or not they would leave the complex or find a place to sleep somewhere nearby, somewhere that they wouldn't get caught.

"I'm not finding him," Jeff said.

"Me, either," Benedict said.

"Hey, Thomas!" Dan raised his voice slightly.

Neyla's eyes were adjusting to the darkness. She made out the shapes around her. The three men, Benedict slightly prone, Dan sitting up, and Jeff, on his hands and knees groping for Ayliffe. The White Tower in front of her. An amazing expanse of ground behind her.

The Grand Storehouse hadn't been built yet nor converted to the Waterloo Barracks. She could see what had been, in Henry III's time, the outer wall, extending all around her. As she turned, she thought she saw movement.

She squinted.

Someone was running silently across the grounds.

Away from her.

"Crap," she said and stood up. "Is that Thomas?"

She pointed toward the shadowy figure.

"It's got to be a guard," Dan said, sounding slightly panicked.

"He's not running toward us," Jeff said.

"Maybe he's getting help," Benedict said.

"No, he's not." Neyla stood and wobbled just a little. Her muscles felt like they'd been stretched and turned inside out. "It's Thomas."

"Why would he run?" Jeff asked.

"He's probably disoriented," Dan said.

"He's not that either," she said.

She should have trusted her instincts.

Thomas Ayliffe aka Thomas Blood.

The damned idiot *had* been sending a message.

And she was finally, *finally* receiving it.

R unning proved harder than he thought. Thomas had fallen hard on his tailbone, knocking the wind out of him. He had lain for a moment on the cool grass.

He had expected the air to stink, but not something

this foul. It was as if he had landed inside a dumpster filled with raw meat on a hot summer evening.

While he tried to catch his breath, he willed his eyes to adjust to the darkness.

The darkness was great luck. He could get to Martin Tower, where the Jewels were kept in the 17th century, with a minimum of fuss, so long as he stayed away from any guards. Then he could take the Jewels, come back somewhere near here, and press his damn remote, all within his three day window.

Hell, if he did it fast enough, he would be inside a three-hour window.

Provided he could stand.

The fall had hurt. He had probably landed on some of the things he'd squirreled inside his linen shirt. He'd brought a paste copy of one of the rings he wanted, as well as some keys and a few small weapons. Tools of the trade, which had probably added to his bruises.

Neyla's voice, sounding musical, American and out of place, asked if everyone was all right. Thomas got onto his hands and knees, stifling a moan as he bent his back.

He crawled along the grass, his fingers finding mud— or something worse. He didn't want to look up. He had no idea how the sewer system worked in the Tower. Did people have privies here? Where did they dump the chamber pots?

He shuddered so deeply that he almost moaned again, but the thought was enough to get him to his feet.

Once on his feet, he could see the outline of the wall built in 13th century. Martin Tower stood on the upper northeast corner, and he could see it vaguely.

He felt disoriented. Knowing that buildings wouldn't be here—the museum for one, the Jewel House for another, Waterloo Barracks for a third—wasn't the same as seeing the grounds without them.

It looked like a completely different place.

It was a completely different place.

He brushed his hands on his knee breeches, grabbed his small bundle of supplies, and started to run as silently as he could.

He headed up the path toward the Martin Tower, ignoring the pain that ran up his spine. His whole body hurt, but he was trying to convince himself that it was the kind of hurt a man got when he had the wind knocked out of him, not when he was seriously injured.

He had to remember the plan.

There would be guards. He had read somewhere, in one of the contemporaneous accounts, that the guards around the Jewels had doubled after Thomas Blood's failed attempt in 1671.

Which was just three years ago now.

Weird.

He had to take out the guards. Break into the Jewel cupboard, and take his items.

If he was really lucky, he would get away completely. Neyla would think he somehow never made it to 1674, and she would go on with her mission without him.

He would complete his theft and be on his way.

With things more precious than gold.

———

Neyla was running before she even realized what she was doing.

She wasn't going to let that arrogant bastard ruin her trip.

She heard one of the men behind her call her name and another shush him. Then she heard footsteps, also from behind her, and hoped it was her team running with her.

She sprinted after Ayliffe. He had too much of a lead for her to catch him, but that didn't matter. Once he reached Martin Tower, he wouldn't be able to get in.

It was locked, and the guards had been doubled in the past three years. He probably didn't know that.

Her breath was coming in small gasps. Her throat tickled. The foul air made her want to cough.

So far, no guards, but that would change. Didn't they hear the commotion in the yard? Weren't they trained to come running?

But she hadn't been able to find out how many guards were on duty in July 1674. Even if she had, it wouldn't have mattered. Corruption was so deep in the Tower that just because someone was supposed to work, it didn't mean that he actually showed up.

She couldn't see Ayliffe any longer. He had to have reached Martin Tower.

Her breath came hard and suddenly she couldn't catch it at all. She wheezed and doubled over, coughing so hard that it hurt. Something was getting to her.

Lack of oxygen. The odors. The smoke.

Something.

Her eyes watered, but she made herself stagger forward.

She had to catch him, before he doomed them all.

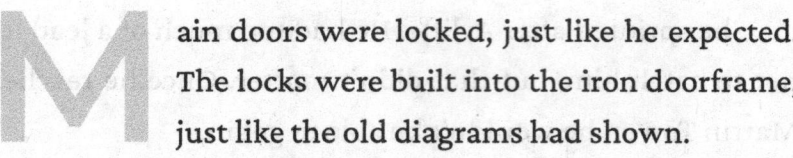

Main doors were locked, just like he expected. The locks were built into the iron doorframe, just like the old diagrams had shown.

He made himself take deep breaths of the thick air. He needed to slow down his heart rate and remain calm.

Then he reached inside his jacket, lifted the edges of his linen shirt, and felt until he found the two tools he would need right now.

The skeleton key, which he had been told was universal, and a teeny tiny stun gun, one that didn't shoot its barbs over a distance. Instead, its business end sent an up-close-and-personal charge through the victims that they wouldn't soon forget.

His hands were shaking. He willed himself to settle down.

He could hear footsteps along the path, then wheezing and loud coughing. He couldn't tell if the cougher was male or female.

Someone wasn't taking well to the 17th century air.

He gripped the skeleton key tightly in his right hand, willed himself to do this right, and stepped in front of the door.

Then he shoved the key into the lock, and turned.

For a moment, he thought it wasn't going to work.

Then he heard an audible click.

"There is a God," he whispered. Or at least, a spirit of some kind, watching over him, helping him succeed.

———————

eyla heard a door creak open. How could the guards be missing this?

What if they weren't?

Dan and Jeff had joined her. She looked over her shoulder. Benedict was only a few yards behind them. He appeared to be running backwards, keeping an eye out behind them to protect them from potential trouble.

She reached the exterior of Martin Tower just as the door creaked closed. Something clicked.

She grabbed the handle and pulled. The door was shut tight.

Locked.

The bastard had shut them out.

Dan caught up to her. He was breathing as hard as she had been.

He tugged on the door, just like she had, and he couldn't get it open either.

"Now what the hell do we do?" she asked.

He grinned at her, then he looked at the windows on the second story.

"We climb," he said.

———

A lantern burned low just inside the door. A guard, sitting on a wooden chair, snapped awake as Thomas turned the skeleton key in the lock.

Thomas started. The guard was wearing the red-and-black Beefeater uniform. Only his was dirty and rumpled.

Thomas made himself take a deep, calming breath. Of course the man wore a Beefeater's uniform. The uniform had been designed in the Tudor era.

The guard spoke. For a moment, it sounded like gibberish. Then Thomas concentrated, like he used to do at the beginning of any Shakespeare play, and the words filtered through his brain.

The man had cursed. His accent was thicker than Thomas had expected, the emphasis on different parts of the words than Thomas had learned.

But they were familiar enough.

The guard stood. He was half a foot shorter than Thomas, and had gone to fat.

He smelled of grease and onions and unwashed flesh.

Thomas's eyes watered. He wondered if he would ever get used to the stinks around here.

"March away," the guard snapped. "Your place is not here."

"Oh, I belong here," Thomas said and pressed his stun gun against the guard's side.

The man burbled, then convulsed, falling backwards to the ground, his head hitting the stone floor repeatedly, sounding like some kind of drum.

Thomas watched for just a moment, making sure the man wasn't having some kind of seizure. The last thing Thomas wanted to do was kill someone.

The guard's face was red, but he seemed okay. He moaned and stopped convulsing. But he wasn't getting up.

He was breathing, though.

Thomas couldn't wait any longer. He grabbed the

lantern off its peg, and hurried down the corridor to the left, hoping against hope that the Jewels were where they were supposed to be.

———

Neyla was still having trouble catching her breath. She looked up. She had free climbed in her training for this mission—part of time travel was getting in the best physical shape possible. But the free climbing she had done had been on fake rock walls in gyms, not on the side of an old stone building.

Benedict caught up to them. "We going in?"

"I am." Dan took a few more steps back, and surveyed the side of the building. "I should be able to let you in shortly after I get inside."

"If you don't get caught," Benedict said.

"O, ye of little faith," Dan said. He gripped the side of the building, then found footholds. "This thing isn't smooth. It shouldn't take me long."

Neyla was glad he didn't ask her to come along. He had asked her to urban free climb back when they were training. She had taken one look at the building that he had chosen in Canary Wharf and immediately declined to go any farther. She realized that afternoon that she had a very mild fear of heights.

He scaled the side of the building like Spider-man

dressed for a Shakespeare play and reached the window in no time at all.

Neyla hadn't even realized she was holding her breath.

He braced himself, then reached into his jacket and removed the knife he had brought with him.

For a moment, Neyla thought he was going to pry the window open. Instead, he used the hilt to smash the glass.

Shards rained down on them. Jeff cursed. Benedict bent over.

Neyla was standing far enough away that she didn't get hit.

"You could've warned us," Jeff said.

She shushed him. They were already making too much noise. She turned and looked at the Inner Ward.

She wasn't sure what she was expecting—exterior security lights to go on? If someone lit a candle a few buildings away, she wouldn't be able to see it.

She turned back toward the building. Dan had disappeared inside.

Now all they had to do was wait.

———

The corridors were narrow and windy, and they smelled of tallow. Thomas kept the lantern in front of him, but it didn't give off much light. Inside the lantern's glass, four candles were carefully braced, but only one had been lit.

The stairs appeared so swiftly that he almost tripped down the first. The stone walls saved him. The walls around the stairs were so narrow that they caught him even as he pitched slightly forward.

His breathing was ragged. He put one hand on the stone wall, wincing at the stone's dampness, and went down.

He would only get one shot at this, especially now that Neyla knew he had no reason to participate in their little bone expedition.

He was glad he wouldn't have to stay here long. He hadn't expected the past to be so creepy.

He followed the twisting staircase down and relaxed slightly when he saw that it opened into a large arched room.

The cupboard was in just such a room—he'd seen someone's portrait of that. He hoped that the ancient art was accurate.

Funny, he had thought it would be easier to break into the Tower without the high level security, the cameras, the motion sensors, the laser traps.

But he had never been so terrified on a job in his entire life.

He walked forward into the darkness, holding the lantern in front of him, and wishing it gave off more light.

———————

Neyla shifted back and forth on her feet. She had shushed Jeff and Benedict more than once, and then they had stopped talking altogether when a man appeared on the west side of the White Tower, slowly walking the Inner Ward.

He held a torch in one hand, but he didn't appear to be looking for anything. It took Neyla a few minutes to realize what he was doing.

He was patrolling the grounds.

She pressed what remained of her little team against the door, and pointed. They nodded. They huddled together as the man walked within a few yards of them, not noticing the broken glass or the three people a stone's throw away.

She hoped he would be gone by the time Dan got the door open.

If Dan got the door open.

She didn't know what would happen if he didn't.

———————

The air down here smelled rank, almost as if the polluted Thames had flowed inside once and no one had bothered to clean it out. The walls and the floor looked clean enough—or clear enough, anyway, since there wasn't any furniture around him.

Thomas held up the lantern, hoping he wasn't hopelessly lost. Then something glinted in front of him.

His breath caught.

He was here.

Finally.

———

The guard and his torch disappeared around the front of the White Tower. Neyla let out a sigh of relief. She stepped away from the door just as something clanged inside.

Then the door creaked open and a thin ray of light trickled out.

"Come on." Dan's shadowy head peered around the door.

Jeff slid in first, followed by Benedict. Neyla entered last, pulling the heavy door closed behind her.

They were in a small antechamber of some kind. Dan had found an old-fashioned lantern, made of iron and glass, designed to protect candles from gusts of wind. The smoke from the candle wisped out of the top, near the metal ring that Dan was holding.

He nodded toward the center of the room. A guard lay flat on his back, his eyes partly open.

"Is he dead?" Jeff asked.

"Dunno," Dan said. "Thought I'd let you in first."

Neyla clenched her fist, then made herself release it, finger by finger. Dammit, dammit, dammit.

Benedict hurried over to the guard and felt his carotid artery for a pulse. After a moment, he said, "He's all right."

That was some consolation, at least. But now, no matter what, they would have to leave. They couldn't show up on the grounds the day a guard was attacked in Martin Tower.

The last thing she wanted was to get caught. Not here. In the 17th century, prisons were foul places, filled with wretched people, particularly the people who weren't wealthy and couldn't pay for their own upkeep.

"What did Thomas do to him?" Jeff asked Benedict.

"Can't tell," he said. "Doesn't look like he was stabbed. Probably hit him over the head."

"Doesn't matter," Neyla said. "We have to find Thomas and get the hell out of here."

"Out of Martin Tower?" Dan asked.

"Out of 1674," she said. "You want to be arrested here?"

"Jesus," he said. "No."

"Where are the Jewels?" Benedict asked.

She had to stop and think. She never studied much about Martin Tower. She knew the history, of course. The Jewels were locked in a ground floor cupboard, beneath the apartments of the Deputy Keeper of the Jewel House.

She had seen drawings of Blood's incredible heist, the one he had nearly gotten away with, and they always portrayed the cupboard as a large space, somewhere nearby.

But to get there directly? She had no idea.

"Was there an apartment upstairs?" she asked Dan.

"There were doors," he said. "I came in a corridor. The lantern was hanging near them. I had to use one of my matches to light it. I hope that's okay."

She didn't care that he had brought illegal matches or that he had lit the lantern. But the fact that it hung near a door not too far from the window meant that the apartments were on the west side of the building.

"We go this way," she said and headed to her left.

———

The light had reflected off a metal padlock someone had hung through the handles of a cupboard. The only cupboard that Thomas knew about was the Jewel cupboard.

This had to be it.

His heart was pounding so hard that for a moment, he

thought someone was coming after him.

He made himself take a deep breath. He would worry about that if it happened. Right now, he needed some jewelry.

He studied the cupboard. The handles, locked shut with the padlock. But the cupboard doors themselves were hinged.

He hadn't brought a metal file, but he did have a few other tools. He could get the tiny nails out of the hinges and pull them off the door. Then the door would open from the side.

It wouldn't take long at all.

He looked around for a place to hang the lantern, found one not two feet away. He stopped, set down his bundle, then removed the candle and used it to light the other three. He replaced them and hung the lantern.

He stepped toward the cupboard and reached for the closest hinge. His hands were shaking.

He had never been so nervous on a job.

He had never done a job as complicated as this.

Thomas forced himself to relax, and slowly, carefully, pried the tiny handcrafted nails out of their hinge.

———

They had gone through a very twisty corridor that seemed to go nowhere.

Neyla was beginning to doubt herself. She usually double-checked things in her research materials or with her computer, but she didn't have fingertip access any more.

She missed it.

She would have missed the stairs too, except that the corridor led right to them. The branch to the right, going away from the stairs, almost seemed like an afterthought.

Dan started going down the branch, but she grabbed his arm and shook her head.

Her memory said the Jewels were on the ground floor, but she wasn't sure how they defined ground floor here. Had her team come in on the ground floor or was there one level down, accessible from another part of the building?

It made more sense for the Jewel cupboard to be as far beneath ground as possible. That way it would be easier to defend.

She started down the stairs.

"I don't think so," Dan whispered. "I think they're on this floor."

"You take Benedict and look," she said. "But first, give us each a candle."

"They're not in holders," he said. "The wax'll burn your fingers."

"I don't care," she said. "I don't see well in the dark."

They stopped. He fumbled with the lantern, handing her a candle and handing Jeff one. Then he closed the glass door and picked up the lantern.

Benedict watched the whole thing as if it were a waste of time.

"If you don't find anything," Neyla said, "come back here. We'll be waiting."

At least, she hoped they would be waiting. She wasn't sure what they would find below. If they did find Thomas, she was going to have to find a way to subdue him. After all, he had almost murdered someone.

She and Jeff went down the stairs slowly.

The stone walls along the side were narrow, cramping her. The walls were damp and the air had a mildewy odor that mixed with the ripeness of stagnant water.

She resisted the urge to sneeze. Something in this time period really bothered her. She hadn't realized she had allergies until she came here.

Still, she made herself move down the stairs as quietly as she could.

When she reached the bottom she saw a series of arches that she recognized from the old paintings.

She was on the right path. She wished she could yell for Dan and Benedict, but she didn't dare.

Instead, she put a finger to her lips. Jeff nodded. Together they walked through the arches, going slowly, hoping against hope that Thomas wasn't planning to ambush them.

———

The wood was groaning, the metal scraping. Who knew 17th century craftsmanship was so damn good.

Thomas took out his knife and started digging into the wood itself. Screw the nails. The wood was the softest part of this damn cupboard. And he was going to get in no matter what.

He was making a god-awful noise. He hoped no one heard it from the apartments above. He knew from the Thomas Blood stories that one of the men in charge of the Jewels—the Keeper of the Jewel House? His deputy?—housed his entire family in Martin Tower.

It had been that family that caught Thomas Blood. The son had inopportunely returned from his military service after years away, and caught Thomas Blood's gang in the act of theft. The gang managed to escape, but the son raised an alarm and the guards caught Blood's gang in the streets just outside the Tower.

Thomas had vowed to himself that he wouldn't get caught.

So far, he seemed to be doing well.

Even if he had to gouge the damn hinges free.

Pounding, cursing, clanging.

Neyla glanced at Jeff, then pointed toward the sound. Two arches away, she could see a soft yellow glow.

Jeff nodded. Then he reached up and pinched his candle out.

Neyla did the same.

They pressed against each other, walking toward the noise.

It had to be Thomas.

She hoped.

Finally, he got the damn thing open. He pulled away an entire door, leaving it hanging from the padlock.

To his surprise, the Jewels weren't sitting on rests or in small holders. They were crammed haphazardly on shelves, looking like nothing more than some very wealthy person's high-end jewelry closet.

He stared for a moment.

He'd seen such riches before. After all, he had seen the Crown Jewels—these Crown Jewels—in their modern display, under reinforced glass with sensors all around, cameras on each jewel, special lighting, and an appropriate setting for each, showing off its sparkling magnificence.

There was no sparkling here, not even when the light caught the diamonds and sapphires and rubies. These things hadn't been cleaned in a generation.

The orb sat to one side. St. Edward's crown, restored after Thomas Blood had crushed it to get it out of the Tower, sat near the back. Thomas couldn't see the Scepter, not that it mattered.

But he didn't want them. He wanted Edward the Confessor's sapphire ring.

He had an exquisite paste copy tied under his shirt. Or at least, what he and the forger thought was a copy. No one knew exactly what the sapphire ring looked like. It had been melted down, the sapphire placed in the Imperial Crown in 1837 for the coronation of Queen Victoria.

All they had to go on were paintings from the National Portrait Gallery and some of those lacked so much in detail that he had been praying he had it right.

Now he realized it didn't matter. The ring was probably as filthy as the rest of the jewelry, and no one knew if there was filigree work or any engravings or anything that made the ring unique.

He should have thought of that. People didn't clean *themselves* in this century. Why would they clean their jewelry?

He went through the cupboard as quickly as he could, searching for the ring.

Each time he found a small piece he could pocket, he moved it to one side. He would take a lot of lesser jewels out of here, things thought sold off to fund wars or lost to the sands of time.

Maybe lost to a traveler in time.

He grinned to himself.

Then he found Edward the Confessor's ring. Thick and well made and surprisingly heavy.

Thomas reached into his own shirt and untied the fake ring. It gleamed compared to the actual treasures.

He tied the real ring inside his shirt, put the fake with the Scepter, and then he looked at the others, trying to figure out how to carry them. He had found five pieces small enough to carry without causing too much trouble.

Counting the ring—which his sponsor saw as the real prize—Thomas would have six pieces. Five for his sponsor (in exchange for Thomas's fee) and one for himself, a keepsake of an extraordinary moment.

But he wasn't done yet.

He would put the other five pieces inside the bundle. He crouched, untied it, and spread it on the floor.

Something rustled near him. A rat? A guard?

He looked up—

And saw Neyla.

H e had jewels. He had come to steal the Jewels, and smart bastard that he was, he took five smaller, lesser-known pieces.

Her gaze met his. He smiled.

"I figure no one will miss these," he said.

"They'd miss the guard," she said.

He raised his eyebrows. "I just stunned him."

"Lucky for you he's not dead," she said.

"I don't think that's lucky. He can identify me. I'm finishing up and getting out of here."

Her mouth opened, then closed, then opened again. Didn't he understand the implications of all of this? Didn't he realize that he had just ruined her trip? That he might get them all killed? Or maybe worse—imprisoned here, in the 17th century?

She shook with fury. "Put those things back."

He smiled again. "And do all this for nothing?"

———

S he launched herself at him.

He tried to duck, but he couldn't, since she had already found him in a half crouch.

She hit him like a linebacker, and knocked him on his

already injured tailbone. Pain swept through him, harsh and unrelenting. He couldn't catch his breath.

She grabbed him by the jaw, fingers behind his ears, and slammed his head against the hard stone floor. Once. Twice. Three times.

He twisted, pain searing through him from his back, then his head, then his back. He wrapped his hands around her wrists and tried to pull her off.

He should buck, but he couldn't get his legs underneath him. They were bent at an angle and he couldn't get purchase.

She was going to kill him. This attractive, monomaniacal bone researcher was so mad she was going to slam him to death.

He tried to gasp out an apology, but he couldn't think clearly enough to put the words together.

He wasn't sure how to stop her.

He wasn't sure if he could.

———

Hands gripped her shoulders, pulling her off.

"You're going to kill him."

Jeff had yanked her back. He was holding her.

Sweat ran down her face. She was coughing slightly.

She had been gripping Thomas's jaw, her fingers digging so hard into his skin that her hands hurt.

Thomas was still on the ground, looking dazed.

If she said she hadn't meant to hurt him, she'd be lying. She had never been so angry in her life. He had hurt an innocent man, ruined years of her work, and threatened all of their lives here in a dangerous past, and he had joked about it.

Joked.

Like it was all one big lark.

She was breathing hard. Then she moved toward him again, but Jeff grabbed her.

"No," he said.

"I'm not going to kill him," she said.

Instead, she dumped out the bundle, then ripped the linen in half.

Thomas had raised one hand to his forehead, and he was moaning. Either she had injured him badly or he figured she wasn't going to attack him any longer.

She handed the ripped cloth to Jeff. Then she grabbed Thomas's hands and pulled them together.

"Tie him as tightly as you can," she said.

Jeff blinked at her.

"Do it!" she snapped. She wasn't sure how long she could hold Thomas.

Jeff tied the linen around Thomas's wrists so tightly that she could see the fabric digging into his skin.

"Now what do we do with him?" Jeff asked.

"Give me a minute," she said, "and I'll figure it out."

For a moment, Thomas thought he was vindicated. Even though his head hurt so badly he could barely move and the pain in his spine traveled all the way through his legs, he figured he would survive this.

When the guards or whoever found him and untied him, he would twist away, grab his little remote and vanish.

He would be gambling that this room would still be in Martin Tower in the future, but it was a small gamble. They usually didn't change the configuration of an existing Tower.

Besides, anything would be better than staying here.

Neyla picked up the Jewels and put them back. Then she stood up, putting one hand on her own spine.

In the other hand, she held his knife.

Thomas's eyes widened. He clearly thought she was going to kill him.

She wasn't going to kill him. She wasn't that kind of woman. She wasn't even going to damage his handsome mocking face, although she was still tempted.

He had no idea how much work he was going to cause her. Somehow she had to drag him out of here. And then they were going to have to deal with him in the future.

She had no idea what would come of that.

But first, she had to make everything right.

She handed the knife to Jeff. Then she untied her own bundle, added Thomas's things to it as she looked for the unauthorized tools he had brought along. Something had gotten him into this building, and he had used something to hurt that guard.

She didn't see anything that would fit those descriptions in his bundle.

Which meant they were on him.

Smart. He might have had to leave the bundle behind. He clearly planned ahead.

She opened his jacket then ripped open his shirt.

The disk rested against his chest. But that wasn't what caught her attention.

What caught her attention was everything he had smuggled in. Skeleton key, extra knife, stun gun, and a dark, dingy ring.

She grabbed the ring.

It was heavy, ugly, and old. She rubbed her finger across it, removing layers of dirt. A gigantic sapphire gleamed up at her.

Edward the Confessor's ring.

But she had seen it in the cupboard.

Gleaming prettily.

Because it came from the 21st century, polished, and shiny. Not because it belonged here.

Because it was paste.

"You son of a bitch," she said. She turned to the cupboard, grabbed the fake ring, and put the original back.

Then she bent over and grabbed the remote, holding it in her hand.

Thomas looked frightened for the first time. "Don't," he said.

"You think I'm going to leave you here?" she asked.

"You can't," Jeff said. "He doesn't fit."

"Don't take that," Thomas said. He wasn't quite begging. She wasn't sure if she wanted him to beg. She didn't want to see him lose all of his dignity.

"Give me one good reason why I shouldn't," she said.

His eyes moved back and forth, as he clearly thought of several options and discarded them. Finally, he said, "You'd be sentencing me to death. You're not that kind of woman."

"Sentencing you to death," she mused. "Here, in the Tower of London."

His cheeks flushed a dark red. She could feel the fear coming off him in waves. He actually believed she might leave him here.

Instead, she let the remote fall back onto his chest.

"Come here, Jeff," she said. "We're going to have to carry him out."

"I can walk," Thomas said.

"So get up," she said.

He rocked, moaned, and was about to work his way up when Jeff grabbed an arm, yanking him to his feet.

"We're not going to let you go anywhere unescorted," Jeff said.

Neyla took the paste ring and all of the tools, putting them in her bundle. Then she left the remains of Thomas's bundle. There was no way to hide the fact that he had broken into the cupboard.

But nothing was missing. So if the guard was smart, he could take credit for chasing the robber away.

Lots of ifs.

She took Thomas's other arm. Then she and Jeff dragged him out of the cupboard room, and back to the stairs.

Thomas thought of fighting, but he was outnumbered, and she had hurt him.

He wasn't sure he blamed her. He had destroyed her life's work.

Damn. He should have escaped. If she had only taken a few minutes longer to reach the cupboard, he probably would have escaped.

If she had been a different kind of woman, he would have asked her to join him. Who could tell if the Confessor's ring was different? He would have wagered no one had tested that sapphire in hundreds of years. Besides, modern paste sapphires weren't made of plastic. They were crystals too, just not quite as valuable as the real thing.

But he knew better than to argue. Besides, what could they do to him? When they got back to the 21st century, it would be their word against his. And even if they convinced the folks at Portals that he had tried to steal the Jewels, it didn't matter. The crime occurred hundreds of years in the past.

No one could prosecute him.

No one would dare.

Or so he told himself as he let them drag him up the stairs, back to the door, and—he hoped—the future.

———

eyla's heart was pounding. Adrenaline still poured through her system. She wanted to move fast, but didn't dare.

The others were waiting at the top of the staircase. Benedict looked terrified. Dan just seemed nervous. He kept turning his head, as if expecting someone to attack them at any moment.

But if no one had come when the guard was attacked, then no one was going to come at all. One thing about thick stone walls. They were mostly soundproof.

Dan took Thomas from her. Neither he nor Benedict seemed surprised that they had captured Thomas or that he looked a little roughed up.

They led him through the corridor as if this had been the plan all along. The guard was still prone. But he had raised one hand to his head and he was moaning.

They had to hurry.

Neyla pushed open the doors. The air outside was cooler but smellier.

It was still dark. Somehow she had expected the sun to be coming up. It seemed like she had been in Martin Tower for hours, and it had probably been less than thirty minutes.

She made Jeff extinguish his candle, then the five of them hurried across the grounds. She kept an eye out for the guard who had made his rounds earlier, but she didn't see him.

When she reached the spot where the team had arrived, she almost told them to get their remotes.

Then she realized that they were feet lower than they had been. They might materialize inside the ground.

For a moment, she felt at a complete loss. The plan had been to find a safe place, figure out the guard schedule, and get out at the right time.

She didn't have time. She had no idea what the right place was now.

The others stared at her.

Then she realized what she had to do.

She opened the bundle and pulled out the skeleton key she had taken from Thomas.

"We're going inside," she said.

They didn't disagree. Because they knew they had no choice.

———

It only took a few minutes to find a door, and get them inside. She was heading to the one place she knew hadn't changed in all the centuries of the White Tower's existence: the Chapel of St. John.

It was up several floors, but she had no trouble getting there. The team ran into no guards, no locked doors. The

White Tower's interior looked pretty much the same now as it would centuries in the future.

The others followed her without question, dragging Thomas with them. For once, he had nothing to say. No quips, no barbs, no suggestions. He just let them take him back to the future.

She wasn't sure she liked this subdued Thomas any more than she liked the arrogant man she had first met. But she wasn't going to worry about him at the moment.

She led the group up stairs and through dingy corridors to the Chapel of St. John. Under the impressive Norman arches, candles burned on the altar. Votive candles, in memory of someone. The Church of England had picked up a lot of habits from the Catholic Church and continued to practice them, for which she was very grateful.

Because the altar itself looked unchanged to her.

She looked at her group. They were filthy from running through dirty corridors. Thomas's jaw had marks from her fingertips. Jeff actually had some blood on his face, but whether that was from her or from Thomas, she didn't know.

"Ready to go home?" she asked.

They nodded.

She would have to untie Thomas so that he could use his remote.

She leaned toward him. "Try anything, and one of us will take that remote and leave you here."

74

He looked up at her. "Have a little compassion," he said. "You're in a church."

She grabbed his remote. "I mean it," she said.

He sighed. "I'll be a good boy."

She nodded. Then she untied his hands.

They all grabbed their remotes. As she nodded, they pressed the activation switches.

And everything went dark.

The wind came up, but it didn't blow hot and cold this time. It blew softly, marking her movement. The smell barely changed either, but maybe she couldn't smell anything after having been in that stinky place.

Then she stopped moving and stumbled against the altar. Jeff stumbled against her. Dan staggered forward, and Benedict fell onto a chair.

Thomas landed in a heap on the floor beside her. His face had turned white. He really was in terrible shape.

No candles burned. Pews extended in front of her and beyond them, one of the Yeoman Warders peered inside.

Her heart jumped.

Had they been caught? Were they going to be arrested?

Then she realized it didn't matter.

The worst thing they had done would be to have stayed past closing time. If the remotes had worked properly, they would have arrived here only a second or two later than they left.

In an entirely different part of the Tower.

"We're closing up," the Yeoman Warder said in very understandable modern British English. "That includes the gift shop. If you want to buy something for home, I'd suggest leaving now. You've got a bit of a walk ahead of you."

"Thank you," Neyla said. Her voice sounded wheezy. She was still lightheaded.

The Warder went back into the corridor, his message delivered.

Jeff grabbed Thomas's arms. Neyla retied his wrists, then leaned against him. "Try anything, and I'll have you arrested."

"For what?" he asked.

"Whatever I can think of," she said, not conceding that he had a good point. What could they do to him? His crime was in the past. Unless he had completed a major identity theft.

Thomas Ayliffe couldn't be his real name.

They secured him. Then they grouped around him— Jeff and Benedict on each side, Dan behind, using his body to hide Thomas's tied hands. Neyla stayed a few yards ahead, just in case something came at them.

They didn't say anything as they trooped down the aisle, out of the chapel, and into the Inner Ward, heading back to the gate.

Heading home.

H e had a concussion, a bruised tailbone, and cracked ribs. Thomas lay on cool hospital sheets where he was being kept for observation. He had a private room, courtesy of Portals, and a security guard, also courtesy of Portals.

He wasn't to talk to anyone outside of the company.

He wasn't sure if that was ever or just for the duration.

All he did know was that the hospital wanted him here for observation since, they believed, he'd had quite a fall when he was urban free climbing with Dan.

As if Thomas would ever do anything that stupid.

He wasn't supposed to close his eyes, but he was tired. Tired and disappointed. So close. He'd actually held the Jewels in his hand. How many modern thieves could say that they had touched the Crown Jewels?

Although touching wasn't nearly enough.

And he wasn't going to be able to go back to his sponsor and make another attempt.

He had failed. His first big failure.

And he doubted Portals would ever let anyone get that close again.

At least he wasn't going to jail. Wycroft had told him that much during his short visit here. Thomas wasn't going to jail because they couldn't prove identity theft and everything else would be "too incredible for any local magistrate to adjudicate."

Thank heavens.

So Thomas, once he healed, would be escorted out of the hospital, out of London, and away from any Portals site forever.

Although he had seen enough of their systems to know that forever might not be that long. Since his sponsor still had people inside, and Thomas did know the system.

He wouldn't get near the Crown Jewels again. At least, not in 1674. And he wasn't going near Neyla.

But if he remembered right, Henry VIII had sold some of the Jewels to pay for his various wars. Maybe, if Thomas figured out the right way to approach things, he could try again.

Years from now.

If he wanted to put in the work.

Which he really wasn't sure he did.

———

Neyla stood in her window, looking down on the Tower Bridge, and the Tower itself.

She would be going back, after she had a ton of allergy shots, once she figured out when would be a good time. She couldn't go anywhere near the first of July, thanks to Thomas. That assault on the guard hadn't made it into the history books and, so far as she could tell, had no impact on history itself. But it would harm her little band if they returned at the wrong moment.

Now, at least, she could wait until Pete was well. She'd have her original team back.

Thank heavens. She wouldn't have to worry about another Thomas Ayliffe.

She had tried to visit him in the hospital, but Wycroft had cordoned him off. Ayliffe was leaving London as soon as he was able, which angered her.

He would be a free man.

Because they couldn't prove identity theft. His identification was rock-solid, no matter how much she believed he had made up the name. They couldn't charge him with corporate espionage, not without divulging a few too many corporate secrets, and they couldn't charge him with any other crime.

In fact, Wycroft pointed out to Neyla, she was the one who faced legal charges. She had assaulted Ayliffe in front of a witness.

In 1674. Because he had made her completely and utterly furious.

She had expected to learn things while in the past. She just hadn't expected to learn she was capable of such violence.

It disturbed her less than it probably should have. She should have been appalled. But she had always known that humans had a base nature. She figured people in the past were closer to it than people of her generation.

But she had proven her own assumptions wrong.

Without that base nature, the Tower wouldn't exist. And she wouldn't have the bones of Princes to investigate.

Maybe she should thank Ayliffe. He had taught her that the past could be dangerous and unexpected—and so could she.

YOU MIGHT LIKE THIS...

THE END OF THE WORLD

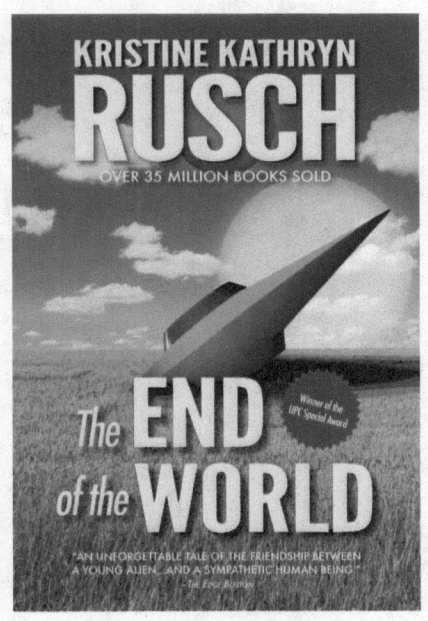

THEN

The air reeked of smoke.

The people ran, and the others chased them.

She kept tripping. Momma pulled her forward, but Momma's hand was slippery. Her hand slid out, and she fell, sprawling on the wooden sidewalk.

Momma reached for her, but the crowd swept Momma forward.

All she saw was Momma's face, panicked, her hands, grasping, and then Momma was gone.

Everyone ran around her, over her, on her. She put her hands over her head and cringed, curling herself into a little ball.

She made herself change color. Brown-gray like the sidewalk, with black lines running up and down.

Dress hems skimmed over her. Boots brushed her. Heels pinched the skin on her arms.

No spikes, Momma always said. *No spikes or they'll know.*

So she held her breath, hoping the spikes wouldn't break through her skin because she was so scared, and her side hurt where someone's boot hit it, and the wooden sidewalk bounced as more and more people ran past her.

Finally, she started squinching, like Daddy taught her before he left.

Slide, he said. *A little bit at a time. Slide. Squinch onto whatever surface you're on and cling.*

It was hard to squinch without spikes, but she did, her head tucked in her belly, her hair trailing to one side. More boots stomped on it, pulling it, but she bit her lower lip so that she wouldn't have to think about the pain.

She was almost to the bank door when the sidewalk stopped shaking. No one ran by her. She was alone.

She flattened herself against the brick and shuddered. Her skin smelled of chewing tobacco, spit and beer from the saloon next door.

She had shut down her ears, but she finally rotated them outward. Men were shouting, women yelling. There was pounding and screaming and a high-pitched noise she didn't like.

If they found her flattened against the brick, they'd know. If they saw the spikes rise from her body, they'd know. If they saw her squinching, they'd know.

But she couldn't move.

She was shivering, and she didn't know what to do.

NOW

The call didn't come through channels. It rang to Becca Keller's personal cell.

Chase Waterston hadn't even said hello.

"Got a problem at the End of the World," he'd said, his usually self-assured voice shaky. "Can you get here right away? Just you."

Normally, she would have told him to call the precinct or 911, but something stopped her. Probably that scared edge to his voice, a sound she'd never heard in all the years she'd known him.

She drove from the center of downtown Hope to the End of the World, a drive that, in the old days, would have taken five minutes. Now it took twenty, and the only thing that kept her from being annoyed at the traffic were the mountains, bleak and cold, rising up like goddesses at the edge of Hope.

Hope was a mountain city, but its terrain was high desert. Vast expanses of brown still marked the outskirts of town, although the interior had lost much of its desert feel. By the time she passed the latest ticky-tacky development, she hit the rolling dunes of her childhood. Even though she had on the air-conditioning, the smell of sagebrush blew in —full of promise.

If she kept going straight too much farther, she'd hit small windy roads filled with switchbacks that led to now-trendy ski resorts. If she turned right, she'd follow the old stage coach route over the edge of the mountains into the Willamette Valley where most of Oregon's population lived.

The End of the World was an ancient resort at the fork between the mountain roads and the old stagecoach route. At the turn of the previous century, some enterprising entrepreneur figured travelers who were taking the narrow road toward the Willamette Valley would welcome a place to rest and recover from the long dusty trip.

Now bumper-to-bumper traffic filled that wagon route, which had expanded to a four-lane highway. Hope actually had a real rush hour, thanks to ex-patriate Californians, retired baby boomers, and ridiculously cheap housing.

Chase was rebuilding the resort for those baby boomers and Californians. For some reason, he thought they'd want to stay in a hundred-year-old hotel, with a view of the mountains and the river, even in the heat of the summer and the deep cold of the desert winter.

Becca steered the squad with her left hand and fiddled with the air-conditioner with her right, wishing her own car was out of the shop. No matter what she did, she couldn't get the squad car cooled. Nothing seemed to be working properly. Or maybe that was the effect of the heat.

It was a hundred and three degrees, and the third week without rain. The radio's most recent weather report promised the temperature would reach one hundred and eight by the time the day was over.

Finally, she reached the construction site.

Chase had set up the site so that it only blocked part of the ever-present wind and as a consequence, the dust billowed across the highway with the gusts.

The city had cited Chase twice for the hazard, and he'd promised to fix it just after the Fourth of July holiday. It looked like he'd been keeping his word, too. A huge plastic construction fence leaned against the old building. Graders and post-diggers were parked on the side of the road.

Nothing moved. Not the cats Chase had been using to dig out the old parking lot, not the crane he'd rented the week before, and not the crew, most of whom sat on the backs of pick-up trucks, their faces blackened with dust and grime and too much sun. She could see their eyes, white against the darkness of their skins, watching her as she turned onto the dirt path that Chase had been using as an access road.

He was waiting for her in the doorway of what had once been a natatorium. Built over an old underground spring, the Natatorium had once boasted the largest swimming pool in Eastern Oregon. There was some kind of pipe system which pumped water into the pool, keeping it perpetually cold. In the Natatorium's heyday, the water had been replaced daily.

Behind the Natatorium was the old five-story brick hotel that still had the original fixtures. No vandals had ever attacked the place. Even the windows were intact.

Becca had gone inside more than once, first as an impressionable twelve-year-old, and ever since, part of her believed the rumors that the hotel was haunted.

She pulled up beside the Natatorium door, in a tiny patch of shade provided by the overhanging roof. She got out and the blast-furnace heat hit her, prickling sweat on her skin almost instantly. Apparently the air conditioner had been working in the piece-of-crap squad after all.

Chase watched her. His lips were chapped, his skin fried blackish red from the sun. He had weather-wrinkles around his eyes and narrow mouth. His hair was cropped short, and over it he wore a regulation hardhat. He clutched another one in his left hand, slapping it rhythmically against his thigh.

"Thanks for coming, Becca," he said, and he still sounded shaken.

The tone was unfamiliar, but the expression on his face wasn't. She'd seen it only once, after she'd told him she wanted out, that his values and hers were so different, she couldn't stomach a relationship any longer.

"What do you got, Chase?" she asked.

"Come with me." He handed her the hardhat he'd been holding.

She took it as a gust of wind caught her short hair and blew its clipped edges into her face. She slipped the hardhat on, and tucked her hair underneath it, then followed Chase inside the building.

It was hotter inside the Natatorium, and the air smelled of rot and mold. She usually thought of those as humidity smells, but the Natatorium's interior was so dry that it was crumbly.

The floor was shredded with age, the wood so brittle that she wondered if it would hold her weight. Most of the walls were gone, the remains of them piled in a corner. Chase had gutted the interior.

When she had been a girl, she had played in this place. Her parents had forbidden her to come, which made it all the more inviting. The rot and mold smells had been present even then. But the walls had still been up, and there had been some ancient furniture in here as well, made unusable by weather and critters chewing the interior.

She used to stand inside the entrance with the door open, the stream of sunlight carrying a spinning tunnel of dust motes. When she closed her eyes halfway, she could just imagine the people arriving here after a long day of travel, happy to be in a place of such elegance, such warmth.

But now even that sense of a long ago but lively past was gone, and all that remained was the shell of the building itself—a hazard, an eyesore, something to be torn down and replaced.

Chase's boots echoed on the wood floor. He led her along the edges, pointing at holes closer to the center. She wondered if any of his employees had caused the holes, walking imprudently across the floor, foot catching on the weak spot, and then slipping through.

He was taking her to the employees' staircase in the back. When they reached it, she saw why. It was made of metal. Rusted metal, but metal all the same. Someone had recently bolted the stairs into the wall, probably under Chase's orders. A metal hand railing had been reinforced as well.

Chase looked over his shoulder to make sure she was following. She caught a glimpse of something in his face— reluctance? Fear? She couldn't quite tell—and then, as suddenly as it appeared, it was gone.

He went down the steps two at a time. She followed. Even though the handrail had been rebolted, the metal still flaked under her hand. The bolts might hold if she suddenly fell through the stairs but she wasn't sure if the railing would.

The smell grew stronger here, as if the mold had somehow managed to survive the dry summers. The farther down she went, the cooler the air got. It was still hot, but no longer oppressive.

Chase stopped at the bottom of the stairs. He watched her come down the last few, his gaze holding hers. The intensity of his gaze startled her. It was vulnerable, in a way she hadn't seen since their first year together.

Then he stepped away so that she could stand on the floor below.

The smell was so strong that it overwhelmed her. Beneath the mold and rot, there was something else, something familiar, something foul. It made the hair rise on the back of her neck.

"That way," Chase said, and this time she wasn't mistaking it. His voice was shaking. "I'll wait here."

She frowned at him, and then kept going. The floor here was covered in ceramic tile, chipped and broken, but sturdy. She wondered what was beneath it. Ground? Old-fashioned concrete? Wood? She couldn't tell. But the floor didn't creak here, and it felt solid.

A long wall hid everything from view. A door stood

93

open, sending in sunlight filled with dust motes, just like she remembered. Only there shouldn't be sunlight here. This was the basement, the miraculous swimming pool, the place that had helped make the End of the World famous.

She stepped through the door.

The light came from the back wall—or what had been the back. Chase's crew had destroyed this part of the building.

The basement of the End of the World was open to the air for the first time since it had been completed.

That strange feeling she'd had since she reached the bottom of the stairs grew. If the basement wasn't sealed, then the stench shouldn't have been so strong. The old air should have escaped, letting the freshness of the desert inside.

Some of the heat had trickled in, but not enough to dissipate the natural coolness. She stepped forward. The tile on the other side of the pool was hidden under mounds of dirt. The pool itself was half destroyed, but the cat which had done the damage wasn't anywhere near it. She could see the big tire tracks, scored deeply into the sandy earth, as if the cat itself had been stuck or if the operator had tried to escape in a hurry.

They had uncovered something. That much was clear. And she was beginning to get an idea as to what it was.

A body.

Given the smell, it had to have died here recently. Bodies didn't decay in the desert—not in the dry air and the sand. Inside a building like this, there might be standard decomposition, but considering how hot it had been, even that seemed unlikely.

She'd have to assume cause of death was suspicious because the body had been located here. And then she'd have to figure out a way to find out whose body it was.

She was already planning how she'd conduct her case when she stepped off the tile onto a mound of dirt, and peered into the gaping hole, and saw—

Bones. Piles of bones. Recognizable bones. Femurs, hip bones, pelvic bones, rib cages. Hundreds of human bones. And more skulls than she could count.

She rocked back on her heels, pressing her free hand to her face, the smell—the illogical and impossible smell—now turning her stomach.

A mass grave, of the kind she'd only seen in film or police academy photos.

A mass grave, anywhere from a hundred to seventy-five years old.

A mass grave, in Hope. She hadn't even heard rumors of it, and she had lived here all her life.

"Son of a bitch," she said.

"Yeah," Chase said from the stairs, "I couldn't agree more."

THEN

T he screaming sent ripples through her. She couldn't complete the change. She couldn't even assume the color and texture of the brick.

Tears pricked her eyes. Tears, as big a giveaway as her hair, her fingers, her ears. Somehow, when she stopped the spikes, she stopped all her abilities.

Or maybe it was just the fear.

A door squeaked open, then boots hit the sidewalk. Polished boots with only a layer of black dust along the edge. Men's boots, not the dainty things Momma tried to wear.

She tried to will the shivering away, but she couldn't.

She couldn't move at all.

Not that she had anywhere to go.

She could only pray that he wouldn't look down, that he wouldn't see her, that she would be safe for just a little longer.

NOW

Becca stared at the hole. She couldn't even count all the skulls, rising like white stones out of the dirt. Not to mention the rib cages off to one side or the tiny bones lying in a corner, bones that probably belonged in a hand or a foot.

She couldn't do much on her own. But she could find out where that stink was coming from.

She turned around and headed for the stairs.

Chase tipped his hardhat back, revealing his dark eyes. "Where're you going?"

"To get some things from my evidence bag," Becca said.

"You're not going to call anyone, are you?" he asked.

She stopped in front of him. "I can't take care of this alone. You should know that."

He leaned against the railing, that assumed casual gesture which meant he was the most distressed. "This'll ruin me, Becca. Half my capital is in this place."

"You told me no good businessman ever invests his own money," she snapped, mostly because she was surprised.

He shrugged. "Guess I'm not a good businessman."

But he was. He had restored three of the downtown's oldest buildings, making them into expensive condominiums with views of the mountains. Single-handedly, he'd revitalized Hope's downtown, by adding trendy stores that the locals claimed would never succeed (yet somehow they did, thanks to the "foreigners," as the Californians were called) and restaurants so upscale that Becca would have to spend half a week's pay just to eat lunch.

"You knew I'd go by the book when you called me here," she said, more sharply than she intended. He'd gotten to her. That was the problem; he always did.

"I thought maybe we could talk. They're old bones. If we can get someone to recover them and keep it quiet—"

"How many workers saw this?" she asked. "Do you think they'll keep it quiet?"

"If I pay them enough," he said. "And if we move the bones to a proper cemetery."

"Is that what you think this is?" she asked. "A graveyard?"

"Isn't it?" He seemed genuinely surprised. "It was so far out in the desert when this place was built that it's possible —no, it's probable—that the memory of the graveyard got lost."

"I saw at least two ribcages with shattered bones, and several skulls looked crushed."

His lips trembled, and it was a moment before he spoke. "The equipment could have done that."

But he didn't sound convinced.

"It could have," she said. "But we need to know."

"Why?" he asked.

She looked over her shoulder. That patch of sunlight still glinted through the hole in the wall. The dust motes still floated. If she didn't look down, the place would seem just as beautiful and interesting as it always had.

"Because someone loved them once. Someone probably wants to know what happened to them."

"Someone?" He snorted. "Becca, the pool was put over a tennis court that was built at the turn of the 20th century. No one remembers these people. Only historians would care."

He paused, and she felt her breath catch.

Then he said, "This is my life."

He used a tone and inflection she used to find particularly mesmerizing. Once she told their couples therapist that with that tone, he could convince her to do anything, and that was when the therapist told her that she had to get out.

"It's a crime scene," Becca said, knowing that the argument was weak.

"You don't know that for sure, and even if it is, it's a hundred years old," he said.

"Then what's the smell?"

He frowned, clearly not understanding her.

"This is a desert, Chase. Bodies buried in dirt in a dry climate don't decay. They mummify."

He blinked. He obviously hadn't thought of that.

"And," she said, "even if they had decayed because of some strange environmental reason particular to this basement, they wouldn't smell after a hundred years."

That guarded expression had returned to his face. Only his eyes moved now.

"Maybe it's something small," he said. "A mouse, someone's lost cat."

She shook her head. "Smell's too strong, and over the entire building. If it were something small, the smell would have faded back when you broke open that wall."

"Not when it was dug up?" he asked, seeming surprised.

"No," she said. "Is that when you first smelled it?"

"That's when they called me."

They, meaning his crew. She frowned at him, wondering if he was going to blame them.

But for what? A smell?

She'd have to find the source before she made assumptions.

And that, she knew, was going to be hard.

THEN

A hand touched her shoulder. A human hand, warm and gentle. Another shivery ripple ran through her. She still had a shoulder; she hadn't gotten rid of that either. How silly she must look, plastered against the brick wall like a half formed younglin.

Screams still echoed. The shouts had died down, although sometimes they rose up altogether, like a group got excited about something.

"You're one of them, aren't you?"

Male voice, human, just as gentle as the hand. She couldn't stop shivering.

"I won't hurt you."

She resisted the urge to rotate an eye upwards, so that she could see more than the boot.

"But you better come with me before they find you."

That did startle her. Her eye moved before she could stop it. It formed above her shoulder. He jumped back slightly when her eye appeared, but his hand never left her skin, even though it was finally turning tannish-red like the brick.

She'd seen him before. Daddy had laughed with him in the good days. He had slicked-back hair and a narrow face and kind eyes.

He crouched beside her, and looked right at her eye, like it didn't bother him, even though she knew it did. He wouldn't've jumped like that if it didn't.

"Please," he said, "come with me. I don't know when they're coming back. And someone might see us. Please."

She had to form a mouth. Her nose remained, tucked against her stomach from when she'd formed a ball, but her mouth had disappeared when she had tried to take on the appearance of the wooden sidewalk.

It took all her strength to make the mouth come out near the eye, and from the look of disgust that passed over his face, she still didn't look right. Her hair was on the other side of her body, and her eye was just above her shoulder. The mouth had probably come out on what would have been her back if she put herself together right.

Right being human.

That's what Momma said.

Momma.

"Please," he said again, and this time, she heard panic in his voice.

"Stuck," she said.

"Oh, Christ." He looked up and down the street, then at the buildings across from it.

He seemed younger than she remembered, or maybe she was as bad at telling human ages as Momma was.

"How do we get you unstuck?" he asked.

She didn't know. She'd never been like this, not this scared, not all by herself.

She tried to shrug and felt her other shoulder form into the wood. A splinter dug into her skin, and her entire body turned red with pain.

"What a mess," he said, and she didn't know if he meant her or what was going on or how scared they both seemed to be.

She willed herself to let go, but she was attached to the brick, and she'd lost control of half her body functions. Daddy said fear would do that.

Whatever happens, baby, he'd say, *you have to trust us. You have to believe we'll get together again. Let that be your strength, so that you never, ever succumb to fear.*

But he'd been gone for a long time now. And Momma hadn't come back for her, even though people were screaming.

The man tried to pry a flat corner of her skin from the edge of the brick. She could feel the tug, saw his face scrunch up in disgust when he got to the sticky underneath part.

"How'd you get there?" he asked.

"Squinched," she said.

"Squinched." He didn't understand. And she spoke his language, she knew she did. She formed the right mouth, she'd been using the words for a long time now, and she knew how they felt inside her brain and out.

"Can you show me?" he asked. "Can you squinch onto my arm?"

She wasn't supposed to squinch to a human. Momma was strict about that. Like there was something bad about it, something awful would happen.

But something awful was happening now.

The screams...

"No," she said, even though that had to be a lie. Momma and Daddy wouldn't forbid something if she couldn't've done it in the first place.

"God," he said, then looked down the street where the screams had come from. Where the shouts had grown more and more angry every time they rose up.

Right now, it was quiet, and she hated that more.

She hated it all.

"Stay here," he said.

He stood up, letting go of her shoulder. The warm vanished, and the fear rose even worse. Her other shoulder disappeared, and she felt the spikes, threatening to appear.

She had to close both eyes and will the spikes away.

When she opened the eyes, he was gone.

She moved the eyes all over her skin, looking for him, and she didn't see him at all.

The street was still empty, and too quiet.

Then, faraway, someone laughed. A mean, nasty, brittle laugh.

She folded her ears inside her skin, and willed herself flat, hoping, this time, that it would work.

NOW

Becca climbed the stairs, clinging to the handrail, the rust flaking against her palms. She had to call for help. At most, she needed a coroner, and probably a few officers just to search for the source of that smell.

But she felt guilty about calling. Chase used to talk about restoring the End of the World when she'd met him. He had brought her out here on their first date, even though she'd told him that she had explored the property repeatedly when she was a child.

Maybe they'd be able to keep this out of the paper, particularly if it turned out to be a graveyard or a dumping ground. But even that probably wouldn't happen.

The newspapers seemed to love this kind of story.

If she reported this, she would condemn Chase's

project to a kind of limbo. With so much capital invested, he probably couldn't afford to wait until the legal issues were solved.

She almost turned around to ask him how much time he could give them, but then she'd be compromising the investigation. For all she knew, there was a recently killed human beneath that dirt, and someone (Chase?) was using the old bones to hide it.

Then she shook her head. Not Chase. He was manipulative and difficult, moody and untrustworthy, but he wasn't—nor had he ever been—violent.

She sighed and continued up the stairs. Much as she wanted to help him, she couldn't. She had an obligation to the entire community.

She had an obligation to herself.

The wind hit her the moment she stepped outside. Bits of sand stung her skin, sticking to the sweat. Even with the sun, it now felt cooler out here because of that wind.

The construction workers watched her. She didn't know most of them; the town had grown too big for her to know everyone by sight like she had when she was a child. Many of these workers were Hispanic, some of them probably illegal.

Hispanics expected her to check their papers. She was supposed to do that too, although she never did. She didn't object to people who worked hard and tried to improve their lives.

With one hand, she tipped her hardhat back and nodded toward the workers. Then she opened the squad's driver's door, and winced at the heat which poured out at her. She leaned inside, unwilling to go into that heat voluntarily, and grabbed the radio's handset.

She paused before turning it on, knowing that even that momentary hesitation was a victory for Chase.

Then she clicked the handset and asked the dispatch to send Jillian Mills.

Jillian Mills was the head coroner for Hope and the surrounding counties. She actually worked the job full time, but her assistants were dentists and veterinarians, and one retired doctor.

"You want the crime scene unit?" the dispatch asked. It was standard procedure for a crime scene unit to come with the coroner.

"Not yet," Becca said. "I'm not sure what exactly we have here, except that it's dead."

Which was technically true, if she ignored all the crushed and broken bones.

"Tell her to hurry," Becca added. "It's hot as hell out here and there's a construction crew waiting."

That usually worked to get any city official moving. Lately, the "foreigners" had taken to suing the city if their emergency or official personnel delayed money-making operations, even for a day.

Chase would never do that—he knew that getting

along with the city helped his permits go through and his iffy projects get approved—but Becca still used the excuse.

She didn't want to be here any longer than she had to.

She stood, lifted her hardhat, and wiped the sweat off her forehead. Then she closed the door and leaned on it for a moment.

The End of the World.

She wondered if Chase had ever thought that the name might have been prophetic.

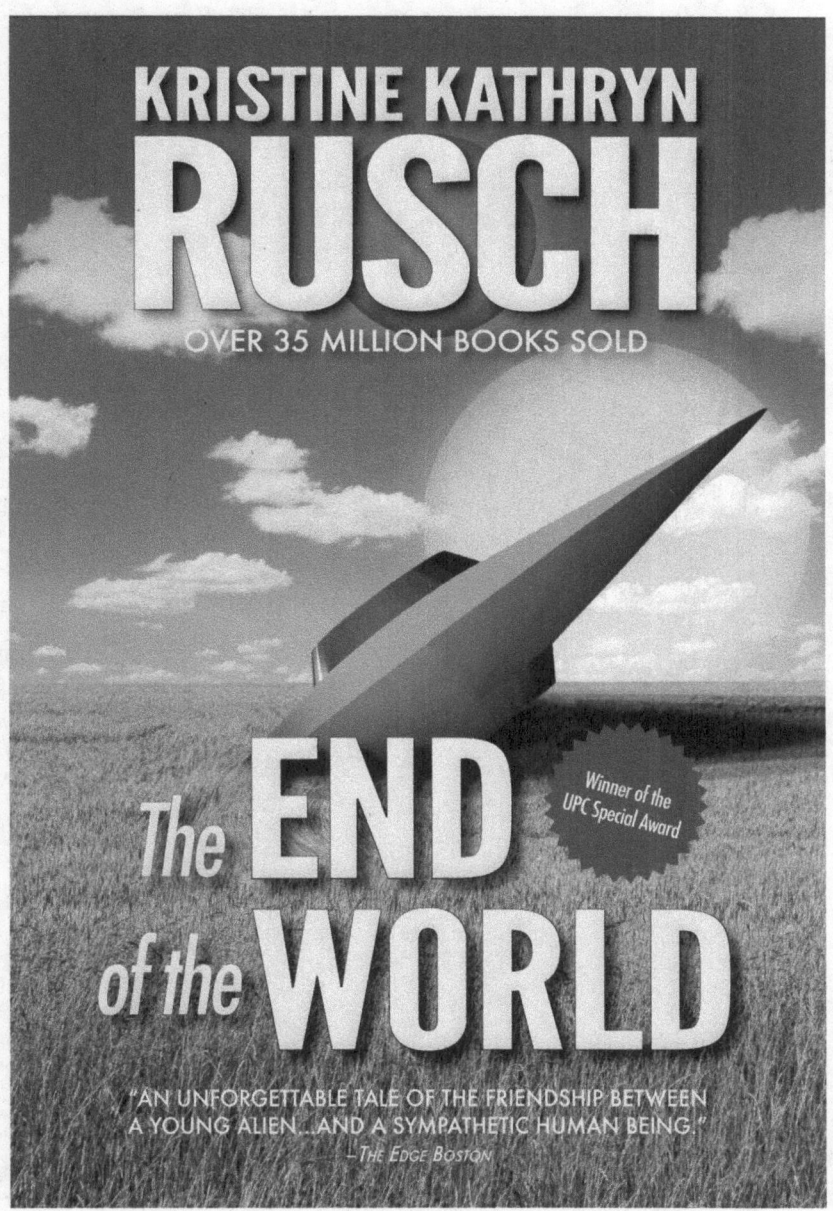

Keep Reading *The End of the World!*

Go to www.wmgbooks.com

HEAR DIRECTLY FROM KRIS

HEAR DIRECTLY FROM KRIS

Sign up for the Kristine Kathryn Rusch newsletter and hear directly from Kris herself.

Go to kriswrites.com.

Get the latest news and releases from all of the WMG authors and lines, including Kristine Kathryn Rusch, Kristine Grayson, Kris Nelscott, Dean Wesley Smith, *Pulphouse Fiction Magazine, Smith's Monthly,* and so much more.

Go to wmgbooks.com.

You can also follow Kris on Bookbub.

We value honest feedback, and would love to hear your opinion in a review, if you're so inclined, on your favorite book retailer's site.

ABOUT THE AUTHOR

New York Times bestselling author Kristine Kathryn Rusch writes in almost every genre. Her novels have made bestseller lists around the world and her short fiction has appeared in eighteen best of the year collections. She has won more than twenty-five awards for her fiction, including the Hugo, Le Prix Imaginales, the Asimov's Readers Choice award, and the Ellery Queen Mystery Magazine Readers Choice Award.

Rusch writes in many genres, from science fiction to mystery, from western to romance. She has written under a pile of pen names, but most of her work appears as Kristine Kathryn Rusch. Her Kris Nelscott pen name has won or been nominated for most of the awards in the mystery genre, and her Kristine Grayson pen name became a bestseller in romance. Her science fiction novels set in the bestselling Diving Universe have won dozens of awards and are in development for a major TV show. She also writes the Retrieval Artist sf series and several major series that mostly appear as short fiction.

Rusch broke a number of barriers in the sf/f field, including being the first female editor of *The Magazine of Fantasy & Science Fiction*. She has owned two different publishing companies, and writes a highly regarded publishing industry blog on Patreon. She also writes a highly regarded weekly publishing industry blog. Find out more about her work at kriswrites.com, and more on all her books at wmgbooks.com.

facebook.com/kristinekathrynruschwriter

patreon.com/kristinekathrynrusch

bookbub.com/authors/kristine-kathryn-rusch

www.ingramcontent.com/pod-product-compliance
Lightning Source LLC
Chambersburg PA
CBHW010737100726
47899CB00009B/3092